SUNSHINE AND SECRETS

The Sisters, Texas Mystery Series
Book 15

BECKI WILLIS

Editing by SJS Editorial Services
Cover by Diana Buidoso dienel96

ISBN 13: 978-1-947686-24-3

CONTENTS

1

He parked the dark-blue sedan near the entrance of the convenience store. It was time for a quick pit stop and a few snacks to tide him over. He needed to settle in before nightfall so he could make a game plan for the week to come.

He knew he looked ridiculous, dressed in a long coat and winter hat, but he couldn't take any chances. No one could recognize him on this trip. He was taking a big enough risk as it was, and the stakes were too high.

He was in and out of the store in a matter of minutes. He had filled up with gas at the last stop and was good to go. So far, the car had lived up to the promise of fuel efficiency, as touted by the man at the car rental place.

Satisfied that the store was busy enough to keep people from staring at him, he felt the much-needed stop had gone well.

Now, to get back on the road and the final stretch of his journey.

Crystal Beach, here he came…

"Well, that was random."

"What's that, honey?" Madison deCordova asked her son as he tossed a bag of chips into the front seat.

Crawling all the way to the backseat of the Expedition, grumbling about long legs in confined spaces, her son didn't answer immediately.

"That dude over there," Blake Reynolds finally said, pointing across the parking lot with a potato chip. "It's seventy-five degrees outside, and he's wearing a full-length coat. With his collar pulled up like that, he looks like he's bundled up for a winter day."

"I know our Texas weather can be erratic, but that's a little over the top," his stepsister agreed. "Maybe," Megan suggested, "he's a snowbird from the north, coming down to check out our beaches. Maybe he's still dressed for the cold."

"Then he hasn't stopped for a break in twelve hours," Blake muttered, "or else he'd have noticed the temperature change and taken off the coat."

"Maybe he just got off a plane."

Beside Megan, Blake's twin sister cocked her blond head to one side. "I don't know," Bethani mused. "He looks sort of suspicious, don't you think?"

"Plane or no plane, he looks like a moron," Blake muttered, "wearing a winter coat in this weather."

Bethani snorted a smart reply. "Takes one to

know one."

"Okay, you two. Knock it off," Madison called back to them. Sometimes they acted half of their eighteen years.

Unfazed by their mother's reproach, Bethani still looked thoughtful. "I don't know. There's just something about him..." She was still working on her mystery theory. Given the household she lived in, it seemed only natural. "He looks like he's up to no good."

Madison took a second look at the man in question. Blake was right. With his hat pulled low and his collar pulled high, it was difficult to see his features. Even as he drove away, he kept his face slightly averted. If he was trying to hide his identity, didn't he realize his outfit made him stand out like an elephant amidst a flock of geese?

She dismissed the idea of him being undercover, even as Blake took new interest in the theory. "Maybe he's a spy. He could be intercepting a package coming into the ship channel."

"He could be sabotaging one of the pipelines," Megan speculated.

"Or stealing a high-tech formula from one of the refineries down here. There's like a hundred of them," Bethani pointed out.

"Or," Blake said, his voice turning conspiratorial. He drew out the word as his blue eyes twinkled. "He could be a hit man with the mafia."

"He does look suspicious," Bethani agreed, "but I'm not sure I'd take it that far."

"I don't know about that." Her twin wagged

his eyebrows. "Our mom *is* known as a dead-body magnet."

"I don't do it on purpose," Madison defended herself. "It just seems to... happen."

"Well, it's not going to happen this trip," her husband said in a firm voice. At the helm of the vehicle, Brash had remained silent as the teens tossed around their theories, but he was compelled to speak up now.

"This is a family vacation," he reminded them. "Our last Spring Break together before the three of you head off to college. I'm off duty for the week, and your mom is taking a break from *In a Pinch*. We're here for fun and relaxation. No mysteries, no conspiracy theories, no dead bodies. Just seven days of sunshine and sandy shores. Absolutely *no* shenanigans."

"That's right," Madison echoed, praying the sentiment would prove true. "No shenanigans."

"Remember you said that," Blake said with a knowing smirk. "Something will happen, and that overactive imagination of yours will put two and two together and somehow come up with five, plus a dead body."

"Not this time," his mother insisted. "I'm on vacation."

Brash made a point to change the conversation. "This place better live up to the hype," he said. "You and the girls have done nothing but rave about *The Mermaid's Retreat* since you came back from that cheerleading competition last year."

"You'll see, Daddy D," Bethani assured him.

"It's totally awesome. Right on the beach, on a quiet end of the island. Well, maybe not island," she corrected herself. "Technically, Bolivar is a peninsula. But it feels more like an island than Galveston does. Galveston is so busy, and with the causeway, you barely realize you've left the mainland and are on an island. Bolivar has more of a laid-back, island feel."

"If it has pretty girls and fishing, that's good enough for me," Blake said.

"I've been to Bolivar plenty of times," Brash said. "Just not to this inn."

"From what I understand, there aren't many inns or motels there," Madison commented. "Most of the rental properties are houses they rent out by the week. Sirenity has one of the few actual bed and breakfasts there."

"A house would have been fine with me, but you seemed to like it there so well when you chaperoned the girls, I thought we'd go back."

"You hear no complaints from me! I loved it there, and Sirenity and I became fast friends. I'm excited about seeing her again."

"You say she runs the place all on her own?"

"Yes, but she makes it looks so easy. I know it can't be, but you can't tell it by watching her. She fixes a divine breakfast every morning, puts out snacks, and nibbles every afternoon."

"You had me at breakfast!" Blake spoke from the back. "But the snacks don't hurt, either."

"Try not to eat her out of business, son," Brash reminded him. "We can buy our own snacks and keep them in the room."

Blake looked mortified. "You can *never* have too many snacks. I say let's eat hers *plus* our own."

"I say be on your best behavior this week," Madison reminded all three teenagers. "I like this woman. I want to be invited back."

"It's a place of business. You don't have to be invited."

"But we could be barred, which had better not happen." Making contact with his eyes, Madison gave him her best mom stare through the rearview mirror. "Got it?"

"I'll be my usual charming self," he assured her with his best smile. "It's easier to impress the girls that way. Which, by the way, I plan to meet plenty of." He smacked his hands together and rubbed them in anticipation.

"I plan to work on my tan for the week," Bethani said.

"Me, too, but I wouldn't mind meeting a nice guy," Megan mused. "Not everyone has a guy like Trenton waiting for them back home."

"What about you, Maddy?" Brash asked. "What's on your agenda for the week?"

"I downloaded five books to my Kindle. If that doesn't keep me entertained, I'll buy more. And you?"

"My number one plan is to relax and unwind. And if fishing factors into that, so be it."

Madison could read between the lines. "So, you definitely plan to fish."

"And, might I point out," Brash spoke loud

enough that everyone could hear, "that not one of us named snooping or stirring up trouble in our plans for the week. Let's keep it that way, shall we?"

The girls rolled their eyes. "Yes, Daddy D."

"Got it, Dad."

"It's your wife you should be worried about," Blake said.

Brash cast her a stern, sideways look. "Maddy? Agreed?"

"I'll do my best," she promised.

"Somehow," her husband muttered, "that doesn't comfort me as much as it should."

Madison remained silent, but she agreed.

Something about that man in the long coat had hit a wrong note. She just hoped their entire trip wouldn't be off tune.

2

The Mermaid's Retreat sat just yards from the pebbled beaches of Bolivar Peninsula. The three-storied inn reached high into the sky, planted solidly upon pillars twelve feet above ground. Most of the area beneath the house was open to the breeze and the views, with parking space around to one side.

Blake let out a low whistle of appreciation when he saw the inn. "I can definitely get used to this for the week!"

"Told you it was great," Bethani said. "You should see the views from the decks!"

"Race you there!"

"What about the luggage?" Madison protested.

"We'll take up what we can carry," Bethani assured her, grabbing the backpack at her feet.

Neither girl took more than their own travel bag. Blake slipped his backpack over his shoulders and grabbed the nearest beach bag before scrambling out of the back and catching up with his sisters.

"Gee, that was sweet of them," Madison said with heavy sarcasm.

"I'll get Blake to help me unload later. Let's get checked in." Brash glanced at the back of the Expedition, which overflowed with luggage and other paraphernalia for their week at the beach. "I just hope there's a lift for all of that," he muttered.

"I trust you and the kids can handle it," Madison assured him with a cheeky smile.

As they took the stairs up to the main level, Brash's knee popped every few steps. It was the remnants of an old football injury that mostly bothered him after long bouts of sitting. He had no regrets, especially when his professional football career led to coaching the best teams in Texas college ball and, eventually, to a job in law enforcement. He was now back in his hometown as chief of police with The Sisters Police Department.

Sirenity Blue was a petite woman with dark, pixie-style hair and a warm, friendly smile. She greeted her returning guests with a hug.

"Madison, girls! How good to see you again." She turned to the men. "You must be Brash. It's nice to finally put a face to the legend. And you must be Blake."

"I question the legend part," Brash said in his pleasing baritone, "but it's a pleasure to finally meet you, as well. Maddy's told me all about you and your inn." He looked around in appreciation. "I can see what she meant."

"In that case, I hope she only had good things to say." Sirenity laughed.

Madison gave her a playfully reproachful frown. "Of course they were good. We haven't stopped talking about this place since we left."

"Then what took you so long to come back?" Sirenity teased.

Madison turned her palms upward in a helpless gesture. She summed it up with one word. "Life."

Sirenity laughed aloud and urged, "Come on. Let's get you signed in so you can get up to your room and relax for a minute. With these three in tow," she tipped her head toward the teenagers, "I imagine it's going to be a busy week."

As the girls hurried to the wall of windows overlooking the water, Sirenity merrily tapped on her computer, asked to swipe Brash's credit card, and asked how many key cards were needed.

"Five," the two guys said in unison.

"You don't want to be captive to the whims of the womenfolk, huh?" the innkeeper asked with a knowing grin. She ran five cards through a magnetic reader, tucked them all inside a small, pocketed folder, and handed it to Blake. "It looks like you're outnumbered, so you can be keeper of the keys." Sirenity smiled, earning a friend for life.

"Finally!" With his flair for dramatics, Blake made a victory gesture. "Someone who understands my plight in life!"

"You're in the Sea-Maiden Pod," Sirenity continued. "It's on the second floor, the corner suite on the left."

Tapping the card holder against his palm,

Blake nodded, approving of her sense of humor. "Sea-Maiden Pod. I get it. If mermaids were fish, a group would be a school. If they were people, they would be a tribe. But if they're sea mammals, they're a pod."

"So much better than calling it the Aggregate Suite, don't you think?" Her blue eyes twinkled in mischief. "Groups of manatees are called an aggregation, and sailors originally mistook manatees as mermaids. Sea-Maiden Pod has a better ring to it."

"I agree." Madison looked at her husband and son. "Ready? You'll have a few minutes before you have to go back down for the suitcases. I'm sure the girls will be asking for their swimsuits any minute now."

On cue, the girls joined them, raving about the sunshine and the tans they anticipated.

"Unless you're a fan of stairs, there's a cargo lift to bring up bags," Sirenity informed the group. "It's around the corner and on the right."

"You, my friend, are a lifesaver," Brash proclaimed.

In a loud whisper, Blake offered a poorly concealed, "Old age, you know."

Brash never missed a beat. "In that case, I'll use the lift, and you can use the stairs." His explanation was easy to hear. "Youth, you know."

Intertwining her arm with her husband's, Madison teased, "Come on, Gramps. I'll help you up to the second floor."

The Sea-Maiden Pod was perfect for a family.

Three bedrooms and two baths flanked a cozy sitting room facing the ocean. As the teens chose which room was the girls' and which was Blake's, Madison wandered into the spacious master.

"Nice room," Brash said from behind her. "Great corner view, too."

"Most of all, a comfy bed!" She was already sinking into its pillowy depths.

He joined her there with a sultry promise. "Where I intend to spend a large portion of our time this week." He pulled her into his arms. His kiss held the same promise.

"Thank you for bringing me here, Brash," Madison said, stroking his auburn hair. She loved the way a few strands of silver shone through, giving him a distinguished look. "Most especially, thank you for bringing the kids along."

"It's not the most romantic anniversary gift ever," he acknowledged, "but with all three of our kids about to leave home and go off to college, I thought we should take advantage of a family vacation while we can."

"I don't even want to think about what happens beyond this week. Let's just call it a family vacation and leave it at that."

"Agreed."

She snuggled deeper into his arms, content with the prospect of sharing a week of stress-free, quality time with her family.

"Didn't I tell you this place was awesome? And that Sirenity was a great hostess?"

"You did. What you didn't tell me was that

Sirenity was so young. For some reason, I was expecting a much older woman."

"I'd say she's younger than us," Madison guessed. "Probably her late thirties."

"And she runs this place by herself? That's a little different, don't you think?"

"Yes, but she seems to have it all under control. I don't think there are a lot of rooms, so I guess that keeps her guests to a manageable number."

"No husband or significant other?"

"Not that she mentioned. Actually," Madison admitted, "to be so warm and friendly, she doesn't talk about herself much. If I remember correctly, she was rather vague with most of her answers."

"I guess she's a private person. Nothing wrong with that."

"But I remember that it did strike me as a bit mysterious. Like there was something she wasn't quite telling..." her voice trailed off in thought.

Brash's stern voice held a warning. "Maddy."

"Not bad mysterious," she was quick to clarify. "I think she runs a perfectly respectable business. But there's something in her past. Something she doesn't like to talk about."

"Again, nothing wrong with that."

"But you do have to wonder—" she began.

"No. No, Maddy, you don't have to wonder," he interrupted her. "This is a vacation. Like I said in the car, no wondering, no snooping, and absolutely no mysteries. We're here to rest, relax, and spend time with our family. Nothing more. Are we clear on that?"

"Aye, aye, cap'n," she said with a faked salute.

Her promise would have been so much easier to keep if she hadn't seen the man again.

Fifteen minutes later, as she held the door open while the guys brought in the luggage, she caught a glimpse of a man's full-length coat. Before she could fully process what she was seeing, the man disappeared into the room down the hall.

Breakfast the next morning was buffet style. Madison and her crew were more than happy with the savory breakfast casserole, thick ham slices, and the wide array of pastries, fruits, and yogurt. Even Blake, aka the Endless Pit, left the table with a satisfied belly.

Madison hoped to see all the inn's guests at breakfast, but only one young couple came in while she lingered at the table. They kept to themselves, whispering and talking lowly to each other. There was no sign of the other man. She wondered if her imagination had been playing tricks on her the afternoon before, or if the man in the mysterious coat was truly staying here at the inn. The odds of that were astronomical, but stranger things had been known to happen.

Brash and Blake were in town renting a golf cart for the week, and the girls were upstairs, changing into their swimsuits. It wouldn't hurt for her to hang around a little longer, hoping to see the other guest.

Swimsuits or not, there would be little actual *swimming* done this week. If the surf calmed and the ocean lay flat, swimming was a possibility, assuming the waters weren't too cold. Even though the sun was shining bright, and the day was warm, the water was a different story.

And if the current were strong and rolling, swimming against the ocean waves wouldn't only be exhausting, but dangerous. There was always the worry of undertow and rip tides.

At best, the girls could play in the gulf water. How far they could wade out depended on the current itself. In waters above the knee, a strong wave could knock a person down.

Often times sand bars, many of them just a few feet off the beach, offered a buffer to the deeper waters. The welcome rise in the shifting sands often resulted in a shallow pool of water, perfect for floating on inflatable rafts, splashing and playing, or sitting in a collapsible chair with toes in the water.

As the tide washed in on foamy lace and left as quickly as it came, the landscape of the water's edge was ever-changing. It was like a game of hide and seek. One moment, the seashells were visible. Just before you could scoop up an interesting specimen, the tide came in and carried it back off to sea. The sand was like quicksand, latching on and slowly pulling intruders into its depths. Toes. Feet. Chairs. Nothing was immune.

Stand still long enough, and the shifting sand would take over. Even the sand bars disappeared at high tide.

There was little danger of encountering a large shark near the shore, but there were sharks, nonetheless. Hunting for shark teeth was a favored pastime, as long as the teeth weren't attached.

The girls promised to wade in water no deeper than their knees, ride low waves on their boogie boards, and to concentrate on finding seashells. Madison had a strong suspicion that their search would extend to scouting for cute guys, as well.

With her family occupied and the dining area empty, Madison enjoyed a few moments to herself. Nursing her cup of coffee, she wandered about, reading some of the framed articles adorning one wall. There were accolades from the Chamber of Commerce and travel blogs, naming the inn the best on the peninsula. She read a brief history of the inn, which was built decades ago as a private home. Hurricane Ike and other major storms had tried their best to take the impressive structure down, but somehow, the house had survived. Storm repairs, renovations, and additional decks gave it an updated look from the original rendering, but it remained an easily recognized icon on the peninsula. Madison especially liked the mermaid weathervane perched on the highest pergola.

There were various other articles, including accounts of the Unnamed hurricane of 1949, Ike, Harvey, and the hurricane of 1900, which still claimed the unenviable title as the deadliest natural disaster in US history. One article told about a deadly explosion at a nearby chemical plant and how it had claimed the lives of many local citizens.

Reading about such destruction was too heavy for this glorious day, so Madison moved along the wall. Among old photographs and historic facts, there was a feel-good story about a young boy on the peninsula who did thoughtful deeds for the elderly, and another on the thought-to-be-extinct Karankawa Indian tribe who once inhabited the area.

Sirenity found her guest there, as Madison studied the articles with interest. The innkeeper approached with a small plate in her hands. "There are only a couple of muffins left. Help me polish them off?"

Madison looked over her shoulder with a mischievous smile. "Perhaps I could be persuaded."

"You drive a hard bargain. What if I bribe you with a fresh cup of coffee?"

"Done."

Minutes later, the two were sipping coffee and enjoying the last of the strawberry muffins.

"These are delicious," Madison said. "Did you make these from scratch?"

Sirenity nodded. "My mother's recipe."

"You didn't hear this from me, but they're every bit as good as Genny's."

"She's your friend who has the restaurant, right?"

"Yes. *New Beginnings*. She went to a culinary school abroad and can make the most amazing pastries you've ever tasted. So, if I say these muffins are as good as hers, that's a *huge* compliment."

"And one that's most appreciated." Sirenity smiled over the rim of her coffee cup.

Madison marveled at the innkeeper's many talents. "How do you do it? How do you run this place all on your own, *plus* serve homemade breakfasts?"

Her new friend laughed. "Lots of prep work, I can assure you. I spend most afternoons baking and prepping for the next day. As for the inn, I have someone who comes in once a week to deep clean and to help get rooms ready for the next guest."

"Well, you certainly make all the rest look easy."

"It's not, but most things of value are seldom easy to obtain."

"You even write fortune cookie quotes," Madison teased.

Her host shrugged. "Just an observation."

Madison wanted to ask about the man in the long coat, but she wasn't sure how to broach the subject. She took another sip of coffee, hoping to sound nonchalant. "I'm sure you meet a lot of interesting people here."

Sirenity's lips curled in a smile. "That's the best part. True, some are more colorful than others, but for the most part, they come as strangers and leave as friends."

"Like me?"

"Like you."

"Do you keep a full house most of the time?"

"I avoid booking at full capacity unless it's absolutely necessary. Sometimes, guests have extended family come in, or a wedding, or something of that nature. But I prefer to keep the numbers small, so I can attend to each guest properly."

"How many rooms do you have? I think I counted six doors upstairs?"

"One is a supply closet. That leaves the suite you're in, four more rooms upstairs, and one on this level. Six rooms in all, which is plenty. Only four rooms are occupied this week."

It was the perfect opening for Madison to indulge her curiosity. "I only saw one couple in here this morning."

"The Raes. They're celebrating their anniversary." Her brow puckered, but she didn't dwell on whatever thought crossed her mind. "There's a family of four checking in today. The other guest didn't join us."

"Ah, that explains it. I thought I saw a man going into the room at the end of our hallway."

Sirenity's slow nod spoke volumes, so much more than her frown had. "That would be Mr. Bob Smith. He requested a tray placed outside his room each morning."

Despite Brash's stern words, Madison's mind kicked into overdrive. Bob Smith? It could easily be an alias. Even though the winter coat was conspicuous in weather like this, it sounded like he was, indeed, hiding something. Keeping to himself reinforced that theory.

From her comment, it seemed even Sirenity found something odd about the man.

"A bit of a recluse, is he?" Madison murmured.

"I'd say that's a fair assessment."

"If that's the case, it makes you wonder why on earth he'd come to the beach over Spring Break."

"My sentiments, exactly. But, who knows?" She shrugged. "Maybe this was the only time he could get away. Maybe he doesn't have kids and doesn't keep up with school holidays. He could have any number of reasons for coming at such a busy time. It's really not my place to judge."

"Nor mine. I guess I just have a curious mind." Madison wrinkled her nose. "Of course, some people go so far as to call me nosy, but curious sounds so much nicer."

"Curious it is, then."

That same curiosity made Madison ask, "How would you classify yourself? Nosy? Curious? Or polite enough to keep your opinions neutral?"

Sirenity contemplated the question before offering an answer.

"I'd say I'm more of a listener. People come here looking for a retreat, but sometimes they need a sympathetic ear. I listen, and I try not to judge. Sometimes, that's all they need to find the answers they're searching for."

Her reply was deeper and more ambiguous than Madison had expected. After a few blinks of surprise, she deadpanned, "And that doesn't leave me curious, *at all*."

Sirenity laughed off the gentle probe for more information. "As much as I've enjoyed our visit, that buffet won't clean itself. I'd better get back to work and let you get back to your vacation."

"No computer in front of me, no clients to

meet with, so this *is* vacation," Madison insisted. "But thanks for visiting with me. Maybe we can find time later to pick our conversation up where we left off."

Sirenity made no promises, just gave a non-committal smile. "Maybe," she said.

Standing so she could clear away what was left of breakfast, the innkeeper politely but effectively put an end to the subject.

3

Bolivar Peninsula was a thin strip of land strung along the upper Texas coast, opposite of Galveston Island. It was comprised of several small, unincorporated communities, including Crystal Beach, Caplen, and Gilchrist. The former had been all but wiped out by Hurricane Ike. Well after a decade, it was finally bouncing back to life.

Although the peninsula was part of Galveston County, not all the rules and ordinances of the main island extended to the twenty-seven-mile stretch of land on the opposite side of the ship channel. Without the restrictions, and unlike on the main island, people were free to drive along the beach here. Automobiles were allowed, but many people preferred more relaxed modes of transportation, such as golf carts, dune buggies, ATVs, and the like.

When the rental company delivered the six-seat golf cart, the de-Reys (Blake's terms for their blended deCordova/Reynolds family) took a ride alongside the watery edges of the Gulf.

"Look at those offshore oil rigs on the

horizon," Blake pointed. "And all those ships, waiting to get into port. Wasn't Galveston like one of the busiest ports in the US for a while?"

A Texas history buff, Bethani answered, "Still is, although Houston's port is even busier. The island was discovered in the 1500s, but it took almost three hundred years before the Mexican government established a port. It turned out to be so busy, the infamous pirate Jean Lafitte created a bustling little village that had a shipyard, saloons, gambling halls, and his own personal mansion, Maison Rouge. The Port of Galveston has been a customs entry port for the countries of both Mexico and the US, and in between, when we were our own country, it was home to the Texas Navy. By the turn of the century, Galveston was the number one port for exporting cotton. Nowadays, it's nicknamed the Port of Everything since that's what it handles."

"Geez," her twin groused. "Thank you for that very in-depth answer to a simple question."

Megan pointed to a familiar trademark floating along the horizon. "That one looks more like a cruise ship."

Bethani gave her brother a scathing look. "Am I allowed to point out that five major cruise lines operate out of Galveston?"

"Yeah, go ahead."

"Thanks. Just did."

Knowing he and Madison would soon miss such petty arguments, Brash just laughed from his seat in the back.

"Hey, Dad," Megan said. "Can we go on a cruise

next vacation?"

Bethani's head bobbed in agreement. "Yeah, Daddy D, that would be a great family vacation!"

Brash hoped to placate them with a vague, "Why don't we just concentrate on our current one and discuss future trips at a later date?"

Megan turned around to give him a stern look. "I know you're hoping we'll forget the idea of a cruise," she said, "but don't count on it."

Ignoring their father's suggestion, the girls chattered about how much fun a cruise would be and the ports of call they would like to visit. Blake drove, slowly weaving his way between sandcastles, kite strings, and pop-up canopies.

"People can camp on the beach?" Blake asked in surprise. They had passed a few vans and motor homes parked near the dunes, but he didn't think much about it until he saw the tents.

"It's public property, so yeah," Brash answered.

"That would be so cool! Jamil and I could come down here one weekend and rough it on the beach." While his sisters planned a much more elegant getaway aboard a cruise ship, he fostered dreams of sandy toes, campfires, and a view that stretched for miles.

"Just beware of the dune rattlers and the island wildlife."

"Wait. Rattlers? The kind that kill?" His eyes met Brash's through the rearview mirror.

"One and the same, so everyone remember to stay on the designated pathways."

"What other wildlife?" Blake wanted to know. "We've been to Galveston before, but it's too populated for much besides pelicans and a ton of sea gulls. Those will pester you to death!"

"Plenty of those here, too, but it's a little more rugged over on this side. Gators aren't uncommon, especially on the bay side. There's also wild boar and coyotes."

"So, the usual suspects, huh?"

"Pretty much."

"I bet all these swamps and bayous make for good duck hunting."

"I've done several hunts down here. The rice fields are great for geese."

"When can we go?" Blake asked eagerly.

"They're out of season right now. And like I told your sisters, let's just enjoy the trip we're on for now."

As they drove along the sands, Madison appreciated the many different styles and flavors on display. The homes lining the beach were a spattering of large and fancy to small and modest, all painted in colors that were either flattering or garish.

The Mermaid's Retreat offered only private access to the beach, but where there were public entrances, Madison noticed the crowds were more concentrated. A couple of food trucks offered tempting treats, and one popular vendor sold flags for people to use on the backs of their vehicles.

Many beach goers had their pets with them, while others were clustered around coolers, rousing games of corn hole, and volleyball nets. Families, couples, and groups of young people mingled side by side, all enjoying the pleasant temperature and the warmth of the sunshine.

Most of the people were dressed in modest attire, although some wore too little to classify as actual clothing. Madison could imagine what Granny Bert would have to say about their scanty outfits. Worse than that, she would probably say it loud enough for all to hear!

But of all those sights and more, Madison didn't see a single soul dressed in a long coat and wintry hat.

As Blake drove, they waved at the vehicles and people they passed. Some called out friendly greetings in return. Others had their music blaring, oblivious to anything other than their own version of fun.

"That's a cute dog," Bethani said, pointing to a big white bundle of energy. "Wonder what kind it is?"

"Who cares?" Her brother grinned. "It's not nearly as cute as the girl on the other end of the leash!" He lifted a hand in greeting to the dark-haired beauty, who returned the gesture with a coy smile.

A pair of motorcycles came from behind, roaring around their golf cart with little room to spare. Blake jerked the wheel to avoid being clipped in the rear.

"What's their problem?" he complained. The front tire of the cart hit a hole in the beach, making them lurch to one side. "Jerks!"

"That's a perfect example of why vehicles shouldn't be allowed on the beach," Brash muttered, helping Maddy right herself in the seat.

"Most people act decent, but there's always an idiot in the bunch," Blake replied, his eyes trailing the motorcycles. The bikes were almost out of sight by now.

"Uhm, we may have another problem," said Megan. "There's a car coming. Better get back on our side."

Even though it traveled at a slow speed, a dark sedan headed toward them.

Blake waited for a little girl to run back to her parents before he steered the golf cart back on course. There were no specific driving rules on the beach, but most people knew to stay to their right. The speeding motorcycles notwithstanding, people tended to obey the universal laws of safety and courtesy.

Seated behind her son, Madison glanced at the oncoming car.

As the vehicle passed, she had a distinct view of a hat pulled low over the driver's face.

Thirty minutes later, they pulled up at the inn. The teens vacated the golf cart as soon as Blake killed the motor, but their parents were slower getting out.

Spotting the blue car parked next to them at the inn, Madison hoped Brash wouldn't notice when she discreetly looked inside. From what little she could see through the window, it looked like the typical rental car, void of anything personal. Not even a discarded coat lay across the seat.

"In case you're wondering," her husband mused in a playful voice, "the engine is still warm. This is definitely the same car we encountered on the beach."

"You noticed that, too, huh?"

In reply, he gave her his infamous smirk. He wasn't a trained professional for nothing.

Taking his cell phone from the pocket of his shorts, Brash snapped a picture of the license plate.

"What are you doing that for?" she asked.

"The same reason you think I am. I'm going to call the office and ask Vina to run the plates. Even though," he acknowledged, "I'm sure it's a rental, and by law, the company can't divulge information about who rented it."

"In that case, find out the rental company and let Granny Bert take it from there. I'm sure she could finagle the information out of even the most straight-laced employee."

"You really shouldn't encourage her, you know."

"You always say that, and yet you never turn down the information she manages to gather," Madison teased.

"But I still don't encourage her."

"Ah, I see where you draw the line!" Madison laughed as she hooked her arm through his and started up the stairs.

"Speaking of your grandmother, what's she doing this week while we're gone?"

"Today, she's covering for Derron in the office. He came up with some story about needing to have his teeth cleaned—for the second time this month, I might add—but you know that means he went shopping."

"Which also means Granny Bert is snooping through your files and hoping to drum up some old business that needs tending," Brash predicted.

"Something like that," his wife sighed. "She and the girls are hoping for some juicy case to work on while I'm gone."

'Girls' was a generous term. None of them— her grandmother, nor her best friends Sybil, Wanda, and Virgie—were under the age of eighty-one. Granny Bert was the heartbeat of the community and had an uncanny knack for knowing *everything* that happened in The Sisters. Between the four, they not only knew everyone in town, but they knew their families, their backgrounds, and what secrets those people only *thought* they were hiding. It was a good thing the so-called Senior Crew of her staff worked for thrills rather than a paycheck; Madison could never pay for the kind of information they provided.

"Maybe it's a good thing I'm not there this week," Brash murmured. "It's probably better for my peace of mind, not knowing what they're up to."

"But is having the man here at the inn with us any better?" Madison wondered aloud. "You have to admit, that's a huge coincidence."

"I'm going with the theory that that's all it is. A coincidence."

"Aren't you the one who said he doesn't

believe in coincidence when it comes to breaking the law?"

"The last time I checked," Brash said, taking the final step to reach the landing, "wearing a coat at the beach wasn't illegal. Odd, but not illegal. Therefore, I'm still going with coincidence."

"I think it's just wishful thinking on your part," Madison muttered as he ushered her through the inn's front door.

He had no time to offer a rebuttal. Madison's phone buzzed in her pocket, and she motioned for him to hold his thought. Seeing her grandmother's name on the screen, she grinned. "Speaking of the devil earlier..."

"I'll be on the deck when you're done," Brash mouthed, brushing his hand along her back. Madison had already spotted the nearest bench to sit on while answering her grandmother's call.

"How's the beach?" Granny Bert asked in the form of hello.

"Great! A bit crowded in parts, but nice and quiet here at the inn."

"Just steer those kids clear of The Zoo," her grandmother warned.

"The Zoo?" She wasn't familiar with the term.

"What they call the rowdier part of the beach, roughly a mile either side of the washout. No place for teenagers to be."

"How do you even know these things?"

"You know our RV group goes down to Galveston a couple of times a year. We usually ride the ferry over to Bolivar for the day, but we know to skedaddle from that part of the beach after dark. Especially the area around the washout."

"Noted," Madison said, nibbling on her lip.

"I called to tell you we already have a job lined up."

"Is this a legitimate job," Madison asked suspiciously, "or something you drummed up?"

"Strictly legit. Banisha Vicker's mom was kicked out of another old folk's home, and she needs someone to sit with her while she's at work, and until she can find somewhere else for her mom to go. I've already talked to the girls, and they're working out a schedule as we speak."

"If I were the one sitting with her," Madison said, "I would wonder why she keeps getting kicked out of senior care and if she's too much to handle. But it sounds like a perfect job for you four ladies, so have at it."

"Already accepted the job and taken a down payment," her grandmother informed her. "We start in the morning."

"Sounds like you've got everything covered."

"We do, so you just forget about the office and enjoy the sunshine. A little sun will do you good."

"I'm about to join Brash out on the deck when we're done talking."

"Don't let me stop you. I'll call if we run into any trouble."

"It sounds like a simple-enough assignment. What trouble could you possibly stir up?"

Madison knew the words were a mistake the moment they slipped from her mouth. With her grandmother and her friends, there was always some sort of trouble brewing. She couldn't call the words back, but she could add a disclaimer. "Wait. Don't answer that. Just do the job, as professionally and efficiently as possible. No shenanigans."

"Madison Juliet Cessna!" her grandmother chided, reverting to calling her by her maiden name. "This woman is our client. We would never pull any shenanigans on her."

Madison sounded skeptical. "We'll see about that."

"Go on and soak up that sunshine," her grandmother sniffed. "I have work to do."

4

Brash eyed the lounge chair, thinking he could go for a little siesta in the warm sunshine about now. Instead, a commotion drew his attention toward the far end of the deck.

"Hey, mister. Why you wearin' that long coat?" a little boy asked.

"Yeah, aren't you hot?" his companion asked. "You look hot. Why aren't you wearing shorts like our dad?"

The two youngsters had the man cornered between them. The man in the coat and hat was literally wedged into the corner of the deck, bombarded by the children's questions.

"You must not be from here," the older of the two boys determined. "You must be a Yankee. My uncle talks funny, and my mom says it's 'cause he's a Yankee. He has a coat that like. He wears it when they come down at Christmas. He lives a long way from us, like Missouri or Montana or somewhere like that."

Brash couldn't help but smile, thinking the

boy was terrible in geography. But there was nothing humorous about the way their questions terrified the man they had cornered. His expression was one of pure panic.

"What's wrong with your face, mister?" the other little boy asked. "It's all scarred. I have a scar, too. Wanna see it? I got it when I went through a barbed-wire fence."

As the little boy lifted his shirt to proudly show off his own battle wound, Brash quickly intervened.

"Hey there, fellas," he broke in. "Sounds like you boys have made a new friend."

"We're trying, but he doesn't say much," the older one complained. His younger brother was still searching for the faint scar across his abdomen. "And he dresses funny, like our uncle."

Brash ran an appraising eye over the cornered man. He had to agree with the boys; the guy did look odd, dressed in his long coat and hat. And he did have a scar on his face. More covered his neck and the back of his hands. But it was his eyes that arrested Brash. They looked traumatized. He sensed it was more than from the boys' line of questioning, which clearly was traumatizing within itself. The man had no clue how to reply.

"That's because," Brash explained, "he just got here, and he hasn't had time to shop for new clothes. If you boys hadn't stopped him, I think he was headed to the store to buy one of these shirts like I'm wearing. Long-sleeved but cool, with just enough UV protection to keep the sun from burning my skin."

"Our dad has a shirt like that." The boy nodded. "But what's UV protection?"

"Why don't you find him and ask him to explain it to you?" Brash suggested.

His younger brother had finally located his scar. "See? Right here! I have a scar, just like your friend!" he beamed.

"That you do, buddy." Brash chuckled. "Now, why don't you boys go find your dad?"

As the boys nodded and skipped away, Brash saw relief flood across the other man's scarred face.

"Kids." Brash hoped the explanation sufficed for the humiliation he had endured.

One curt nod from the man acknowledged the sentiment.

"You might want to find you a different hat, too," Brash offered. "One with a floppy brim, like a fishing hat."

The man's voice was rough as he offered a grunted 'thank you' without looking Brash in the eye. He hurried away as quickly as he could, leaving his rescuer with a frown on his face.

Brash still wore the frown when Madison found him. He stared intently at the ocean, oblivious to her approach.

"You look like you're stalking a shark," she commented. "What's going on?"

"Huh?" Her presence took him by surprise. He whirled around, saw her there, and the frown on his face relaxed.

"What's up? Why do you look so serious?" Madison asked.

He hesitated a moment before answering. "Something odd just happened."

Her gaze went down to the water. "Oh?"

"Not down there. Up here."

Madison glanced around, seeing nothing unusual around them. Down the way, two young boys were playing hide and seek behind the deck chairs while their father lounged on one of them, half-watching their antics, half-checking for holes in his eyelids. She assumed they were the newcomers Sirenity had mentioned.

Seeing nothing odd about energetic little boys, she turned back to Brash. "What happened?"

"I saw the guy."

"What guy?"

"The one from yesterday. The one in the dark-blue sedan."

"Mr. Smith?"

Brash arched his brow. "Is that his name, or just what you decided to call him?"

"It sounds better than 'the man,' don't you think? But yes, that's his name. Supposedly." Seeing her husband's expression, she quickly went on, "*Bob* Smith, no less. That definitely sounds like an alias to me."

"Or his parents didn't have much imagination," Brash countered.

"Sirenity says he's very reclusive. Between the name, the clothes, and the way he stays to himself, I'd say he's definitely hiding something."

"Or it could be because of the scars."

"What scars?"

"The ones on his face. And on his neck and his hands. Those are just the ones I could see. Who knows what's under all the clothes?"

"You got that close to him?"

"I not only got that close to him, but I also talked to him."

"What? Why didn't you say so to begin with?"

"I'm saying so now," he replied in his maddeningly calm way.

"Well? What did he say?" she asked in exasperation.

"Very little. One word, in fact." He went on to explain his encounter with the mysterious Mr. Bob Smith. "Those little boys over there cornered him and asked why he was dressed like that at the beach. They asked why he wasn't wearing shorts and why he had scars on his face."

Madison's eyes widened. "What did he say to that?"

"Nothing. They didn't give him a chance. They just asked one question after another, and the younger one wanted to show off his own scar. I could see the guy was mortified, so I stepped in and tried to smooth things over. He didn't seem to know how to answer such direct questions."

"You know kids. They don't have any boundaries at that age. They're just being curious, not cruel."

"They're honest, that's for certain," he agreed wryly.

"What did you say to them?" she asked. "How did you handle it?"

He relayed the conversation, concluding with, "That young couple who's staying here came out about then, and you could tell they were trying to listen to the conversation. The only thing he said was a muttered thank you to me and high-tailed it out of here."

"Wow. I feel a little sorry for him, with all those scars and all."

"I know. Maybe that's why he wears a coat," Brash speculated.

"That was very nice of you, saving him further embarrassment and giving him pointers on a better way to dress. The UV protection should protect his sensitive skin."

Brash looked back out at the waves. "Yeah, but now I'm wondering if that was the right thing to do."

Madison knew what he meant. "Because you still feel uneasy about him?"

He nodded. "There was something in his eyes…"

"See? You're as bad as me!" Madison couldn't help but gloat. "You see a mystery behind everything."

"You have to admit, a man with that many scars, wearing a full hat and coat in this kind of weather—at the beach, no less—is rather mysterious."

"Exactly what I said! To which you said, and I quote, 'no wondering, no snooping, and absolutely no mysteries.' Your words, Brash," she accused, poking a finger into his arm. "Not mine."

"Maybe I stand corrected," he mused, looking

back out at the ocean. "Or maybe," he said, crooking an arm around her waist and pulling her against him, "I should take my own advice and remember I'm on vacation with my beautiful wife and our three amazing kids."

Madison smiled and accepted his kiss. They remained at the railing, enjoying the view and the warm ocean breeze, until the girls interrupted them.

"There you are!" Bethani said in exasperation. "We thought you'd gotten lost."

"Just enjoying the view," Brash assured her.

"We wanted to know if we can meet up with some friends this evening and hang out on the beach."

"What friends?" Madison asked. "Is someone from home down here, too?"

"No, we just met them yesterday," Megan explained. "You probably saw us talking to them down on the beach. Patty and Lindsey are roommates at Sam, and they're here with Lindsey's family and their neighbors. We haven't met the others yet, but there's a couple of other teenagers in their group."

Bethani saw the way her mother's eyes narrowed in thought. "I know what you're thinking, Mom. That Sam Houston should offer a degree in partying, cause that's what most of the students do. But these girls seem pretty grounded. And they're just freshmen, so legally they can't buy alcohol if that's what you're worried about."

"They seem really nice, Mama Maddy," Megan added. "They invited us to play beach volleyball and then have a weenie roast down by the water. It's just a few barrels down, so we won't be very far away. And nowhere near The Zoo." She referred to the trash barrels placed at intervals up and down the beach. Each was numbered, offering a point of reference for location.

Her stepmother gave them a perceptive look. "So, you know about The Zoo, do you?"

"Mo-om." Bethani rolled her eyeballs. "Of course, we know about The Zoo. And we definitely know not to go down to the washout after dark."

"Good. And don't let anyone talk you into it, either."

"We're not morons," Megan pointed out. "We have good heads on our shoulders. And Blake will be there, too, so we can be accountable for each other. Would that work?"

Madison looked over at Brash. "What do you think? They just met these girls."

"I think," Brash answered in his irritating, rational way, "that this fall, they won't be asking our permission to hang out with new friends. Like it or not, sweetheart, our babies aren't babies anymore."

Both girls flocked to his side, hugging him from either side.

"You're the best, Daddy D! Thank you." Giving him another squeeze, Bethani turned back to her mother. "And we promise to behave, Mom. Like Megan said, we aren't morons."

"I know that. And I trust all three of you. It's these other kids I'm not sure about." She went on before Bethani could interrupt. "But your father is right. You're about to be out on your own, and we have to trust your judgment. Just stay with the crowd and have your phones with you. No wandering off in the dark, even with a cute guy."

"*Especially* with a cute guy," Brash added.

Blake had come up sometime during the conversation and overhead most of what was said. With a grin, he propped his arm across his mother's shoulders and asked, "Does that mean I can wander off with a cute girl?"

"Absolutely not. The same rules apply to you, too, buster."

"Yeah, yeah, yeah," he playfully grumbled.

"At least with us out of your hair, the two of you can have a nice, quiet, romantic evening," Megan pointed out.

"But," Blake reminded them with a twinkle in his blue eyes, "no wandering off in the dark. You never know what's out there lurking in the shadows."

5

While the kids were having a good time on the beach, Brash ordered takeout from a local seafood restaurant. He and Madison ate on the deck, savoring a bottle of wine and the soft southerly breeze. The sounds of the ocean and the starry night sky above added special magic to the evening.

"I think," Brash said, covering her hand with his, "we should have one more glass of wine." As his voice slipped to a slow, sultry drawl, he added, "But not out here on the deck. I was thinking somewhere more private."

"As in… that big cushy bed?"

"Exactly like that big cushy bed."

Sometime later, fully relaxed but unable to fall asleep, Madison slipped from the bed where her husband slumbered. The kids weren't in yet, and the mother hen in her needed to know her brood was back in their nest.

Dressing in her lounge pants and a soft tee, Madison quietly left the suite. She was afraid she might wake Brash if she stayed on the top deck, so she took the stairs down to the main floor. Grabbing a bottled water from the cooler Sirenity supplied for guests, she crossed the lobby and stepped into the fresh ocean air.

She didn't see her at first. Her hostess was seated near the rail, just beyond the circle of light. As Madison's eyes adjusted to the moonlight and the soft glow of the fairy lights hung below deck, she saw her friend.

"Mind some company?" she asked as she approached.

Sirenity smiled and indicated the chair beside her. "Have a seat."

"It's a beautiful night," Madison said, climbing into the high seat and settling in.

"So, why aren't you enjoying it with that handsome husband of yours?"

"We had a lovely dinner out on the deck earlier, just the two of us. He's already gone to bed now, but I couldn't sleep. The kids are still out, hanging out with some new friends they met, and I just..."

"Need to know they're safe," Sirenity finished for her. "I get it."

"Do you... have kids?"

"No," she admitted. "No, so maybe I don't know exactly how you feel, but I think I can come pretty close." She turned to stare back out at the ocean, a look of pain filling her face.

Madison's tone was soft. "Who is it?" she asked. "Who do you wait for?"

Without looking her way, Sirenity asked, "Am

I that transparent?"

"I know the look."

She was slow to answer. When she did, her voice sounded exceedingly sad. "It was a long time ago. I waited. And I waited. But he never came back." She cleared emotions from her throat. "The ocean had claimed him."

Madison's heart ached from the pain she heard in the other woman's voice. "I'm so sorry," she whispered.

"Like I said, it was a long time ago."

Madison didn't call her on the weak denial. It was obvious Sirenity still wasn't over the loss. She must have loved the man deeply.

They sat in silence for a while. While Sirenity stared out at the waves, Madison scanned the beach for signs of the kids. She knew they were almost adults. At eighteen, the law said they were. But her mother's heart added the *almost* misnomer. In her eyes, the twins were still her babies, and even though she hadn't given birth to Megan, she loved her like her own. She couldn't help but worry about them.

She knew all three teens were very responsible for their age. They weren't known for reckless behavior or making bad choices. Yet there were so many variables tonight... an unpredictable ocean... a dark sky... new friends who might not share the same sense of responsibility. And, if she were being realistic, alcohol. It could easily be the recipe for disaster.

Stop it, Madison, she told herself. *Don't look for*

trouble where none exists.

She had almost convinced herself she was overreacting when movement in the shadows caught her eye. She sat up straight in the chair, trying to see what—or who—moved down below. The movement was just beyond the dim halo of light, appearing fuzzy and indistinct. But she stared long enough, and hard enough, to discern the shape of a person.

"Madison?" Sirenity asked. "What's wrong?"

"Uhm, maybe nothing. But I see someone down there in the shadows."

"That's not so unusual. A lot of people like to walk along the beach at night."

"In the shadows?"

"Yeah, some of them." Sirenity shrugged. "Maybe they're on a late-night rendezvous. Maybe they're just seeking solitude. People have their own reasons."

"But the way they're moving... It's like they're deliberately staying in the shadows. Like they're doing something wrong and trying not to get caught."

"Again... rendezvous, solitude..."

"I don't think so," Madison murmured. "This looks secretive."

Now curious herself, Sirenity leaned up in her seat. "I don't see anything."

"Over there. See? You can occasionally see the dim glow of what looks like a cigarette."

Sirenity squinted her eyes for a better look. "Yeah. Yeah, I think I do."

"Anyone you recognize?"

She studied the shadowy blob. "I don't think so."

The person moved on, until the shadow was no longer visible. Madison was hesitant to ask, "Do you think that could have been Mr. Smith?"

Sirenity's gaze lingered on the now-vacant spot. "I don't think so," she decided. "I saw Mr. Smith going up to his room just before I came out here. He was sporting a new look: long-sleeved fishing shirt, light-colored pants, floppy hat. It looked like the person down there was wearing shorts."

Madison smiled. "It sounds like he took Brash's advice."

"What do you mean?"

She relayed the incident to the innkeeper as Brash told it to her.

Sirenity nodded in approval. "That was a very nice thing for your husband to do."

"He's sort of awesome that way."

Her friend gave her a teasing look. "Try not to brag too much."

"I know, I know. I have a bad habit of hiding how proud I am of my husband. But that's so like him. He has this innate way of making people feel comfortable, no matter the situation. Even when..."

Sirenity waited for her to go on. When Madison didn't, the innkeeper prodded, "Even when..."

"Even when he's not sure he did the right thing."

"I guess I don't understand."

"You said yourself that Mr. Smith—if that's even his real name—could be described as a recluse. But, scars or not, it just seems odd that he came to the beach if he planned to stay bundled up the entire time. He didn't buy the appropriate clothes until Brash suggested them."

"I still don't understand your point."

"Brash can't help but wonder if he did more harm than good. I mean, what if Mr. Smith is here to harm someone? What if Brash just helped him blend in, so he can ambush someone, or do them harm?"

Sirenity didn't answer right away. Gently clearing her throat, she said in a quiet voice, "I don't think you have to worry about that."

Madison gave her friend a sharp look. "You know something about him that we don't?"

"Not exactly," the innkeeper admitted. "But I just have this... feeling... about him."

"About him? Or for him?"

"What? No, of course not! I never met the man until he checked in yesterday."

"Then how can you sound so positive that we have no reason to worry?"

Sirenity looked back toward the water. The moon had come out from behind the clouds to reflect off the dark waves. "It's complicated."

"You didn't let my 'even when' comment slide. I'm not letting this one slide, either," Madison said. "What's so complicated?"

Sirenity cocked her head to one side, still staring at the ocean, as if deciding the best way to answer.

"This morning," she finally said, "I told you I was a listener. But I don't just listen to a person's words. I listen to their body language. I listen to what they *don't* say, more than what they do."

"I'm trying to improve my skills on that," Madison said wistfully.

"It's more than that. I can… sense… things about people. I can't really explain it, other than to say I listen to people's souls."

Madison looked at her with skepticism. She didn't believe in the supernatural. "You're saying you're clairvoyant?"

"I think the correct term is that I'm intuitive. I'm sensitive to what people are thinking, what they're feeling."

"So, you're good at reading people." This, she could wrap her head around.

"That's part of it, yes. But—and I know this probably sounds crazy to you—but I seem to have a talent for drawing people to me that are in need. Most of my guests come here looking for something. They don't always know what that is, but I help them figure it out."

"Like you said, you're a good listener. He probably said something when he made the booking, or when he was checking in…"

"Mr. Smith, if that's his name, has probably said less than two dozen words to me. Yet I'm certain he came here for something other than a vacation. He's lost something that's important to him, and he's trying to make amends. Don't ask me how I know this, but I do."

At Madison's silence, Sirenity sighed and shook her head. "I shouldn't have said anything. Just forget it."

"That's a little much to forget, don't you think?"

"I get it. I do. Most people are skeptical about things they can't explain. Even *I* can't explain it. But it's real, nonetheless."

"It's not that I don't believe you..."

"Yet you don't." Sirenity moved to push from the chair. "I think I'll turn in. The door will lock behind me, but your key card opens all outside doors, as well."

Madison put a handout to stop her. "Please, don't go. I want to understand this, I do. It's just... a lot to comprehend."

"I know. It sounds crazy, and I have no evidence to back me up on this, but I somehow know that Mr. Smith is full of pain and regret, and that he came here to seek forgiveness."

Madison's analytical mind searched for another answer. "Maybe, the scars..."

"Not all scars are visible, Madison," Sirenity chided softly. "Call it what you like. Intuition. Listening skills. Empathy. A knack for connecting with people. Whatever it is, it's real, and people come here to find peace. This inn, and the answers I help some guests find, is my calling in life."

Madison murmured, "You said that the first time I met you."

"In many ways," Sirenity confided, "this inn saved my life. It gave me hope. It gave me purpose.

And now I use this inn, and this sense of purpose, to help others." She let the words settle between them before she spoke again. "Please believe me when I say Mr. Smith doesn't need doubts and suspicion. He needs help."

"What—What kind of help?"

"I don't know yet. But the answer is here, and I'm listening for it."

Patty Roberts was the quietest one of the group that gathered on the beach. While the rest of her friends laughed and played, she sat back and watched. Her eyes strayed as much to the shadows as they did to the volleyball net.

Sometimes, the girl lamented, she felt like an old person trapped inside a young woman's body. She was too young to shoulder the burden she felt, but she had nowhere to turn for help.

For as long as she could remember, it had been just her and her mom. When her parents divorced, the two of them moved to a small little house in Lufkin. Patty had very few memories of her father. At times, her watered-down memories felt more like fantasies. She thought she remembered a smiling man throwing her up in the air and catching her in a sure, strong grip. She remembered giggling and begging him to do it again. Or maybe it was all in her imagination. A warm thought to comfort her when her mother was too tired and too sad to play with her.

Patty knew her mother loved her. Loretta

Roberts did the best she could for her daughter, but it was hard to raise a child on her own. She worked two jobs just to make ends meet.

Before Patty started kindergarten, she went to the daycare where her mom worked. She spent afternoons there throughout her elementary years, but by high school, she was on her own until her mother came home, exhausted and out of sorts after listening to kids cry and bicker all day. And when she was home, Loretta worked her second job, taking in odd sewing and mending projects. She had a talent for alterations and turning old garments into new, sought-after creations.

The two jobs were enough to support their simple, if not meager, lifestyle, but Patty knew her mother could never afford to send her to college. Sorely aware of that fact, Patty devoted herself to her studies and graduated at the top of her class, earning a scholarship to Sam Houston University.

Patty felt a little guilty at first, going off and leaving her mother all alone. But Loretta insisted she couldn't be prouder of her daughter, and it gave her more time to work on her sewing projects. She had a few pieces of her revamped garments on consignment at a small boutique, and a bridal store had hired her to make alterations for them. It helped Patty to worry less, but soon, she had a new worry.

She had no concrete evidence to take to the police, but Patty was certain someone was stalking her. No one called her phone, only to hang up the moment she answered. No one left her notes or creepy flowers outside her door. No one approached her in darkened hallways or at the parties her friends sometimes dragged her off to. But occasionally, she saw a shadow around the corner, or caught the faint whiff of a cigarette. The tobacco had a very distinct scent to it and one not exactly unpleasant. As a rule, Patty hated cigarette smoke.

But she *felt* someone watching her, so she knew they were there.

She knew it wasn't because she was a raving beauty. She wasn't like her roommate. Lindsey had a gorgeous smile and a figure that most girls, Patty included, could only envy. Lindsey drew people to her like a moth to a flame, whereas Patty was content with a weak flicker.

Just like tonight, when all the other kids were out there having fun.

Patty couldn't be so carefree. She couldn't enjoy that sense of abandon, that pure exhilaration of sand, surf, and smiles as wide as the starry Texas sky.

Because she knew he was out there.
She felt him watching her.

6

THE SISTERS

Long before the vacationers gathered for their breakfast buffet, Granny Bert and her friends had showed up at the Vickers household bearing a basket of assorted baked goods.

They had decided a meet and greet would be best for Ella Getty. That way, she would already be acquainted with each one of them when they showed up on an individual basis.

Banisha greeted them at the door, appearing breathless and a bit haggard.

"I'm glad you're here. Mom is being especially difficult this morning, and I have to leave for work soon. I haven't even fed her breakfast yet."

"We've already taken care of that," Granny Bert said, indicating the basket. "Just give us an overview of what we need to do, and we'll take it from there."

"Like I told you over the phone, my mother can be quite a handful at times. It hasn't always been that way, but about four years ago, she fell and hit her head. She hasn't been herself since. She's argumentative, opinionated, and, honestly, sometimes downright mean."

"You're saying that's a bad thing?" Granny Bert cracked.

"Plus, don't believe a thing she tells you," Banisha went on. "She makes up the craziest stories and convinces herself they're true. She really should have been a writer because she has a very vivid imagination."

"Doesn't sound too bad." Wanda shrugged. "If nothing else, she'll keep us entertained."

"You just have to watch her," Banisha warned. "She'll try to push all your buttons and bully you into getting what she wants."

"If anyone can handle her, it's us," Granny Bert assured the younger woman. "It sounds like we all have something in common."

Their client smiled. "That's why I was so relieved you would be the one sitting with her. She needs a firm hand."

"Just show us the ropes and get on to the bank, before Joe Glenn thinks he's lost a teller."

Banisha was more than happy to explain what she needed from them. She had a list of instructions, numbers, and her mother's likes and dislikes already on the counter. Within ten minutes, she had introduced them to Ella, kissed her mother goodbye with a stern warning for her to behave, and had gone out the door.

Ella Getty was a small woman with stooped

shoulders, heavily wrinkled skin, and a haunted look in her eyes. It wasn't the empty stare of a person on the verge of dementia. Her eyes were full of painful memories and a sadness so heavy, it sank down to her toes.

"Ella, you are in luck today!" Granny Bert declared, clapping her hands together. "These ladies here are some of the best cooks in Rivers County. Wanda's made a batch of her zucchini bread that's sure to make you weep. Virgie whipped up her famous quiche balls, and Sybil made biscuits. They're so light and fluffy, you'd better hold on to one or else it'll float away. And these are my prize-winning apple muffins. We'll brew up a pot of coffee and get plates. Do you like to eat in here, or in the kitchen?"

"I prefer my room," Ella huffed, "but my daughter insisted I come out and meet my new babysitters."

"Like the rest of us, I reckon you passed the baby stage a few years back," Granny Bert said smoothly. "We're your new companions."

"You sayin' I'm old?" the other woman challenged.

"I'm saying that every single one of us in this room is inching our way toward the century mark. Between us, that's a whole heap a lot of experience. And a lot of stories, too. If nothing else, we can swap stories and recipes to pass the time. You much of a cook?"

"Used to be, back when they let me live in my own house and have my own stove." Her voice was filled with bitterness. "These days, my daughter thinks I'm too daft to light a burner. That girl grew up on some of the finest eatin' in the countryside, and now she thinks she's too good for down home cookin'. She wants everything to have some fancy name and cost three times what it's worth. That girl is living above her raisin', I can tell you that!" Ella Getty huffed.

Granny Bert cackled in glee. "We are going to get along just fine, Ella. Just fine, indeed."

While Wanda and Sybil left to prepare coffee and the breakfast tray, Granny Bert and Virgie visited with their new charge. The conversation was going well until an odd expression crossed Ella's face, and she barked, "Gracie! Gracie, what's taking so long with that coffee?"

Virgie slid a sideways look to her friend. "Ella," she addressed the woman across from them in a calming tone, "none of us are named Gracie. Sybil and Wanda are the ones making the coffee. I'm Virgie, and this is Bertha."

"I know who y'all are! I'm talking to Gracie. Though a lot of help she is, leaving me sitting here starving half to death and with no coffee a'tall this morning!"

"There's no Gracie here, Ella."

"Guess I'll have to fire her, too. You just can't keep good help these days!"

"Well, now, lucky for you we're here to help out now," Granny Bert said. "At least until you can replace Gracie."

"Don't want to replace her," the woman

snapped. "I'm doing fine on my own."

They were saved from replying when Sybil brought in a coffee tray. Wanda trailed behind, carrying plates and napkins.

"Breakfast!" Sybil announced cheerily. "Shall we eat at this table?"

"That's where I do my jigsaw puzzles," Ella informed her.

"Well, I don't see a puzzle started yet, so let's have our breakfast here this one time. Is that okay with you?"

Ella agreed, if not somewhat grudgingly. She needed no help standing from her chair and maneuvering her walker into the living room.

"Banisha insists I use this thing," she grumbled, "even though it's useless."

"I heard you had a nasty fall a few years back," Virgie said. "I'm sure she's just being helpful."

"I fell because the ladder collapsed with me, not because I was too feeble to walk on my own."

"I took a tumble off a step stool just a few days ago," Granny Bert commiserated. "The trick is not to let your children know about it. They can be such worrywarts at times."

"*I* didn't tell them about it," Ella insisted. "It was that nosy ambulance driver who went and blabbed."

"I've had the same problem myself." Wanda nodded. "Get a little tipsy over margaritas, knock over a couple of chairs, fall into the lap of another diner, and they think you've had a heart attack or something. They call an ambulance, and then the driver wants to call the next of kin. There's no privacy these days and certainly no respect."

"If you'd learn to hold your liquor," Granny Bert harrumphed, "you wouldn't need an ambulance."

"I didn't need it then, either!"

Loss of appetite was not one of Ella Getty's ailments. She piled one of everything on her plate, plus a healthy portion of fruit, and was doing a good job of polishing it off.

"This bread reminds me of Gracie's," Ella said, savoring the taste.

"Your cook made good zucchini bread, did she?" Virgie asked as a conversation started.

"Gracie wasn't my cook."

"Your maid, then."

"She wasn't my maid, either. She was..." She stopped, looking suddenly confused. "I don't remember what she was, but she made zucchini bread just like this. My pappy grew more zucchini than we could eat, so she made up a bunch of loaves and froze them for the wintertime."

Sybil, always the peacemaker of the bunch, made light of Ella's lapse in memory. "So, your father was a farmer?" she asked. "Where are your people from?"

A change came over Ella, and her face hardened like stone. "I don't talk about that."

Sybil blinked a few times in surprise. "Oh," was all she said.

"Here." Granny Bert thrust another biscuit her way. "Aren't these the lightest biscuits you've ever bitten into?"

"They'll do." Her words were nonchalant, but they all noticed how quickly she snatched the treat from Granny Bert's hand.

After a while, Virgie made another stab at conversation. "I hear you've had a run of bad luck with the nursing homes lately."

"They keep kicking me out." Ella made no bones about it.

"I have the same problem at the casinos," Wanda sighed. "They have too many rules and regulations."

"Same way at the old folks' homes. Course, nowadays, they like fancy titles like senior living, or care facilities. Still the same thing."

"I take it you don't like them?" Virgie asked.

"Of course not! They kept telling me what to do and when to do it. Wanted me to stay in my room all the time. Didn't understand that a soul needs sunshine and fresh air to survive."

"Amen to that," Sybil agreed.

"Acted like God didn't give me two legs for a reason. Threw a fit every time I went for a walk, especially if it was at night. Made me wear a bracelet that beeped if I went very far."

"That's no way to live," tsked the sympathetic other woman.

"And they wouldn't let me in the kitchen to show them how I like my eggs," Ella further complained. "They used some fake, slimy mess they poured out of a cardboard carton. Tasted like cardboard, too. And instead of using hogs for bacon, they used a durned old turkey! The food in those places is worse than any hospital's!"

"Count me out, then," Wanda said. "I love me some fluffy scrambled eggs and good, crisp bacon that comes straight off a hog's belly."

"My pappy raised hogs, too," Ella reminisced. "We never went without pork, and plenty of it."

"See? I knew you were raised on a farm, same as me." Sybil smiled.

Ella's face once more turned to stone. "I told you. I don't talk about those days." She shoved back her plate. "It's almost time for my morning shows. If you really want to help, y'all can clean up and let yourself out."

"Actually, I plan on sticking around today and keeping you company," Granny Bert said.

"I don't want company."

"Then I'll just watch TV with you or do some knitting. Do you like to knit?"

Ella rolled her eyes. "Don't tell me we're going to have craft time here, too!"

"Only if that's something you want to do."

"It's not. I hated it there; I'll hate it here."

"Then no craft time."

Ella settled into her easy chair and used the remote to turn on the television. While she watched game shows, the other women cleaned up the kitchen.

"This may be harder than we thought," Wanda confessed. "She's a cantankerous old biddy, isn't she?"

"I think it's like her daughter said. She's

pushing our buttons. Testing her limits, so she'll know how far she can push," Granny Bert speculated. "All four of my boys used to do the same thing."

"What is with her and the mood swings?" Sybil wanted to know. "She's the one to bring up her father and then jumps down my throat if I ask any questions."

"Keep your throat intact and don't ask questions," Virgie suggested.

"But now I'm curious. Why keep bringing him up if she doesn't want to talk about him?"

"Maybe it's part of her memory problems."

"I'm sure glad I still have my memory," Wanda commented as she dried off the last plate. Between the four of them, the work hadn't taken long.

"Please!" Virgie huffed. "You can't ever remember where you parked your car. Or if you were even driving. Last week, you kept looking for your old rattletrap, even though you rode with me to WalMart."

"For the first two minutes, *you* helped me look!" she shot back at her friend.

"We're going to have our hands full enough with that one in there," Granny Bert predicted, hitching her thumb toward the living room, "without arguing among ourselves."

Wiping the counter dry before folding the hand towel and setting it aside, Virgie deemed the kitchen done. "Well, I wish you luck today," she said. "If you need reinforcement, give us a call. Surely one of us can relieve you."

"I'm sure I'll do fine, even if I have to hog-tie her to her chair."

Halfway through her morning shows, Ella fell asleep.

With nothing to do, Granny Bert was bored out of her mind. After she dusted the shelves in the living room, prepped for lunch, and swept the kitchen for the second time, she finally sat down for another cup of coffee.

"Is that all you do?" Ella's voice jarred Granny Bert from her thoughts. "Sit around and drink coffee all day?"

"Only when the game shows on TV become unbearable," Granny Bert replied flippantly.

"Sassy, aren't you?"

"No more than you, I'd say."

"I wasn't always this way, you know," Ella confessed. "I was happy once upon a time. But then things changed... There's no going back, not after something like that happens."

Her new companion looked at her with curiosity. "Like what, exactly?"

"Like something I don't want to talk about!" Ella snapped. "Can't you just let it be?"

Granny Bert studied her for a moment. "I can. The question is, can you?"

"You expect me to just forget?" Her tone was incredulous.

"I have no idea, because I have no idea what you're talking about."

"Let's leave it that way."

Granny Bert made no reply. She let the silence speak for her as she drank the last of her coffee.

Yep. This assignment wouldn't be as easy as she first thought.

After lunch, Ella asked if they could sit outside on the back porch.

"I don't see why not," Granny Bert agreed. "Like you said, fresh air and sunshine is good for the soul."

Once settled, Ella seemed content to look out over the expansive backyard.

"Once upon a time," she reminisced, "all this area right here was a garden. The soil was just right for growing squash, zucchini, peas, even pumpkins in the fall. We always had a bumper crop."

Granny Bert knew better than to mention Ella's father. There was a nice bit of acreage surrounding the house, meaning it could have easily been part of a farm at one time. The house was obviously old, leaving her to wonder if Ella had actually grown up in it. She didn't recognize the other woman, but there were a few people, especially those who had lived out in the country, that she hadn't known. Not many, she was pleased to say, but a few.

"I can see that," she said agreeably. "My brother Jubal has a farm similar to this. Grows some of the best crook neck squash in the county."

Ella made a sound of disbelief. "Not better than my pappy's." She lifted a finger to point. "See that spot over yonder? That's where the well was.

Sweetest water you ever did taste. And that tree yonder?"

"The big pin oak?"

"That's the one."

"What about it?"

"Don't ever go near it," Ella cautioned. "It's evil."

"How can a tree be evil?"

"Because that's the tree where the bodies are buried."

It didn't happen often, but Granny Bert was left speechless.

She stared at the other woman, who seemed completely unaware of her outlandish statement. Was this one of those wild tales Banisha had warned them about? Or was she simply referring to an animal's body—that of a family pet, or a favorite plow mule, or some casualty from a haplessly launched slingshot? She hated to admit it, but Granny Bert was too spooked to ask for clarification.

She texted a group message to her friends.

What do we know about Ella Getty? Is it possible she grew up here?

Virgie was the first to reply.

Don't remember her, but I guess it's possible.

Sybil added,

If she did, it was when she was a little girl. Don't recall anyone by that name in recent years.

Wanda made it a consensus.

I don't think so, but I can ask around. Why?

Granny Bert reply was vague.

Just something she said made me wonder.

While they sat on the porch enjoying the breeze and the sounds of nature, Ella drifted back to sleep. Content to stay where she was, Granny Bert didn't feel the need to get up and move about this time.

After a good thirty minutes, Ella started talking in her sleep.

"No," she mumbled. "It's not right." Her next several sentences were incoherent, a jumble of grunts, moans, and protests, mingled here and there with a soft snore. But there was no denying her sharply spoken, "No! Not Gracie!"

Hoping to break the hold of the nightmare she was caught up in, Granny Bert gently shook her arm. "Ella? Ella, why don't we go indoors now? You can take a nap in your own bed."

"Huh? Wh—What?" she asked, sputtering awake.

"I said why don't we go in now? You fell asleep in the chair. Don't you think your bed would be more comfortable?"

"I don't deserve to be comfortable," the other woman moaned.

"Of course you do. Now, come with me. We'll get you inside."

Finally awake, Ella's eyes strayed back to the oak. "Evil," she whispered. "Pure evil."

That afternoon, Ella was even more difficult than she had been that morning. She insisted she didn't want to take a nap. She wanted to do a jigsaw puzzle. Why wouldn't her *babysitter*—she spat the word—let her have one? She would report her to the head nurse for elderly abuse. And where was her sweet tea? She always had sweet tea in the afternoon. Gracie knew exactly how she liked it. Where was Gracie? Why wasn't Ella allowed to see her? She demanded to see Gracie, right this minute!

She didn't make any more outlandish claims, but her behavior was bad enough.

By the time her daughter arrived to take over, Granny Bert didn't think to ask Banisha any questions.

For once in her life, she was simply too exhausted to snoop into someone else's business.

7

Madison hadn't quizzed the kids when they came in the night before, but she did the next morning over breakfast.

"How was your volleyball game and weenie roast last night?"

"Fun! We had a great time," Megan said.

"That's mostly because she met someone," Bethani teased.

Megan shot back with, "So what?" a little too defensively. "We all met him. He's nice."

"And cute, if you go for that tall, broad, athletic type."

Madison wiggled her brows, sliding her gaze over to Brash. "I know I do," she said. Eyes back on Megan, she asked, "So, what's his name?"

"Brandon. He's best friends with Lindsey's neighbor, and both of them go to Texas A&M."

"There was no sneaking off to the shadows, was there?" Brash asked.

"No, Dad. I barely know the guy."

"No rolling eyeballs at me, young lady," he

scolded in jest. "What about the rest of you? Have fun?"

"Oh my gosh, it was so much fun!" Bethani said. "We had a total blast!"

"Blake?"

"I'm with them. Beach volleyball, pretty girls in swimsuits, a bonfire with hot dogs... what's not to love?"

"Pretty girls, huh?"

"It's hard to decide which one's prettier. Patty, Lindsey, or Rachel. And the guys were cool, too."

"Rachel is...?"

"Josh's younger sister. And before you ask, Josh is the neighbor. And then there's Lance, Lindsey's older brother."

"So... two brother/sister duos, and two best friends."

"You catch on quick," Blake teased his mother.

"Did you meet the parents?" Brash asked.

"Nah, I think they were having a party of their own, smoking weed and downing shots."

Seeing the looks on their parents' faces, all three teens burst out laughing.

"Gotcha!" they said in unison.

"We knew you would ask," Megan said, "so we decided to have an answer ready."

Bethani nodded. "Sometimes parents can be so predictable."

"Sometimes teens can be so annoying," her mother returned.

"Well, I'm glad you had a good time," Brash told the kids.

"There was one weird thing that happened last night," Blake offered with a frown.

"Oh? What's that?"

"There was this guy. Older dude. Not the one we saw before. At least, I don't think so."

Brash frowned. "What was he doing?"

"Just standing there. He stood far enough away that I couldn't really see him well, but I knew he was there."

"How did you know that, if you couldn't really see him?"

Blake scrunched up his nose. "I could feel him staring at us, you know? And every once in a while, I saw the ring of light from his cigarette."

At Madison's sharp intake of breath, Brash sent her a questioning look.

"I saw someone like that last night in the shadows," she said.

"When?"

"After we went to bed, I couldn't fall asleep. I finally got up and came downstairs to sit on the balcony down here, so that I wouldn't disturb you. Sirenity was out here, and we had a long talk." She gave her head a tiny shake, trying to push thoughts of that conversation out of her head for now. It wasn't relevant to this conversation. "While we were sitting there, I saw someone in the shadows. And it looked like they were smoking a cigarette."

"What was the person doing?" Brash asked.

"At first, I think they were just standing there. But then they started moving, and soon, they had completely blended into the shadows."

"Do you think it was our mysterious Mr. Smith?" Brash asked in concern.

"Not according to Sirenity. She felt rather strongly about that, as a matter of fact."

"How so?"

Not wanting to get into it just now, and especially not in the public dining room, Madison hedged, "For one thing, she said she had just seen Mr. Smith go up, and he wasn't dressed like the person in the shadows. The guy we saw was wearing shorts."

"So, it was a guy?" her husband confirmed.

"I think so. I mean, I don't know for certain since it was so dark, but I got that impression. By the time the moon came out from behind the clouds, he was long gone."

"I think the guy I saw was wearing shorts, too," Blake said.

Bethani nodded. "I think I saw him, too. It felt like someone's eyes were on us."

"Maybe it was one of the parents." Brash gave the kids his infamous smirk. "Maybe they weren't so high that they couldn't slip down and make sure everyone was safe."

"It felt creepier than that," Bethani said.

"But I thought you kids were further down the beach," Madison reasoned. "Are we sure this was the same guy?"

Brash shrugged. "I guess we can't be for sure, but it sounds like it's definitely possible."

"Or, it could be two random cases of perverts out for an evening stroll," Megan offered with a fake smile, "watching from the shadows to get their jollies."

"When did you become so cynical?" Brash asked his daughter.

"You've always taught me to be conscious and aware of my surroundings. Like it or not, Dad, there are a lot of weirdos out there. Girls, especially, have to constantly watch for that kind of thing."

"At least you were listening to me," he muttered.

"How can I not? You drill it into me every time I leave the house."

"Me, too," Bethani seconded.

Brash nodded. "I'm just trying to keep you safe. I didn't intend for you to become jaded."

Fingering the handle of her coffee cup, Madison wondered if she, too, had become cynical. Sirenity had confided in her, yet she had listened with a closed mind.

She made a mental note to become the kind of listener her friend obviously was.

"What is it we're doing again?" Bethani all but whined as she dangled a heavy string into the water. They were on the bay side of the peninsula off the Intercoastal Canal, standing on the banks of one of the marshy inlets.

"Crabbing," Brash replied.

"Where's our hooks?"

"We don't use hooks," he explained. "All we need is a string tied around bait."

"But we're using chicken necks."

"That's the bait," he told her. "The crabs will nibble on the chicken and when you feel a tug, you very slowly pull in the string. Move too fast, and you'll knock them off, so you have to be slow and steady."

"How do we get them up on the bank?"

"We scoop them up with a net."

"Like this!" her brother said. Megan already had a crab on the line, and he was scooping the net inside the water, pulling it out with its bounty. "Look at this! A nice blue crab on her first try!"

Bethani felt renewed enthusiasm for the sport. "I want one, too!"

"Then keep an eye on your line. When it goes taut and you feel something tug, you probably have one."

"I'm not sure I—wait! I think I felt something!" In her eagerness, she pulled the string too hard, and the crab got away.

"Slowly, Beth. Slowly," Brash reminded her.

Brash coached her through her next attempt, which resulted in a crab too small to keep. Still, Bethani insisted on taking her picture with the spry little thing before it scurried away and escaped into the water. After several more attempts, she finally had a keeper.

Madison laughed at her daughter's excited squeal. Not so very long ago, her daughter wouldn't have been caught dead standing in a marsh, fishing for crab with a simple white string and a chicken neck. When they had lived in Dallas, Bethani's idea of fun was shopping at the mall with her friends or letting Grandmother Annette show her off at the country club. Madison hated to admit it, but her daughter had been somewhat of a snob. Moving to The Sisters was the best thing that could have happened to her daughter.

Of course, it hadn't really been anyone's choice to leave Dallas. But after Gray died, Madison discovered they were all but broke. She sold their house at a loss, paid off what debts she could, and moved home to Juliet to live with her grandmother. It had been hard on all of them, especially Bethani. Blake had adjusted easily enough, but Bethani had been such a Daddy's girl. She took his death especially hard and put up a huge resistance when her mother started seeing Brash.

Looking at them now, it was hard to remember those difficult days. Not that she really wanted to. A part of her would always love her first husband, but their marriage had died long before his fatal car wreck made her a widow. It had been more than his infidelity that killed their marriage, although that was the final straw. Over the years, Gray had become more focused on building his career than he was on building their family. They had grown apart and couldn't seem to find their way back to one another.

And even though Madison had loved Gray, she had never loved him the way she loved Brash. As cheesy as it sounded, Brash completed her, and she had never been so happy. Watching Bethani interact with him now, laughing and smiling up at him like an adoring daughter, made her heart swell even more. Blake had always been closer to Brash than he had ever been to his biological father, but Bethani's love hadn't come so easily. Brash had been patient, first earning her trust and her respect, before eventually earning her heart.

"I have another one!" Megan called. "Come on, Mama Maddy! Scoop 'er up for me!"

Megan, at least, had accepted Madison easily enough. She had been Bethani's first friend in the new town and a frequent guest at their house, long before their parents started a relationship.

Madison still marveled at how her archrival in high school, Shannon Wynn, had raised such a smart, loving daughter. Even though Shannon and Brash were only married for two years, they had done a remarkable job co-parenting their child. It had also come as quite a surprise to Madison to discover that Shannon wasn't nearly as terrible as she had always believed. The two of them had become good friends. There was no rivalry between them now, just a shared love for the auburn-haired young beauty named Megan.

"Hurry up!" Megan urged her. "It's a big one."

They both laughed when Madison scooped the net down into the water and a dainty little crab fell through the weave.

"He may have been little," the girl admitted, "but he put up a good fight."

"You'll get a better one next time."

"As long as we're having fun," Megan said, "does it really matter?"

"Are you? Having fun, I mean?"

"I'm having a blast! This entire week has been great!"

"We've only been here two and a half days," Madison laughed.

"Then just imagine what the next five will be like."

"I like your optimism," Madison agreed. "How about a selfie of just the two of us?"

"To go in my baby book?" Megan teased.

"Something like that. Now smile for the camera."

"Hey, a little help over here?" Blake interrupted their cozy mother-daughter moment. "I need the net."

Madison hurried over to him, helping him scoop up a decent-sized crab.

"What about you, Mom? Aren't you going to try your luck?"

"I'm having fun watching you kids."

"Here," he offered. "Take my string. No reason you can't get in on the action, too."

After thirty minutes, the crab stopped biting and they decided to call it a day.

"What are we going to do with the crabs? Cook them?" Bethani wanted to know.

Brash peered inside their bucket. "Not enough for a mess. Looks like we'll have to throw them back out."

"After all that?" she protested. "All that work for nothing?"

"It wasn't all work. It was a lot of fun, too,"

Brash pointed out.

"Okay, you got me there. It was fun," she admitted. She bent down to tip the bucket toward the water. "Go on, you pretty little blue creatures. Back into the wild to live another day."

"I'll tell you what. I'll take everyone out to eat to make up for it," Brash offered. "There's a great place in Galveston that specializes in crab."

"Can we go right now?" Blake wanted to know. "I'm starving!"

"I don't think they open until four. Why don't we find something here on the peninsula, instead? It will be faster than riding the ferry over to Galveston."

"Deal. The faster, the better."

"I swear you have a hollow leg where you stash all that food," Brash muttered. "Come on, family. Let's gather up our stuff and find somewhere to eat."

8

After lunch, they spent the afternoon on the beach.

It was a gorgeous day to be there. The breeze was just warm enough to ward off any chill blowing in from the water. The overhead sky was a perfect blend of fluffy clouds and sunshine.

Brash had erected a pop-up canopy for shade, but for now, they were soaking up the sun. It was also a good way to dry off after they had all waded knee-high into the water. The kids had a good time splashing their mother with water, and Blake had challenged Brash to a swim. Fighting the incoming waves, they swam several yards out until Brash, easily in the lead, declared they had gone far enough. Anything more would pose a real danger.

Blake admitted defeat and collapsed on the beach blanket beside his sun-bathing sisters. He rejuvenated when he spotted their newly made friends.

"Hey, look," Blake said. "There's the girls." He made a megaphone with his hands and called out,

"Yo! Over here!" Helping gain their attention, his sisters waved wildly to their friends.

"Hey," a pretty brunette said as they approached.

"What's up? Where's the rest of the gang?" Blake asked.

"They went fishing," another answered. "Some charter boat or something."

Blake turned to look at Brash. "Hey, Daddy D. Can we do that? Charter a fishing trip?"

"I have a buddy who offered to take us out on the bay," Brash said, busy drying off with a towel. "He said to name the day."

"Today works for me!" Blake's blue eyes lit with excitement.

"Let's give him a little more notice than that." Brash chuckled. He looked at the girls. "Are these the new friends you told us about?"

"Yes!" Megan answered. She and Bethani had already gotten to their feet. "Girls, meet our parents. Or, as we call them, Daddy D and Mama Maddy. These are our new friends, Rachel, Patty, and Lindsey, in that order."

"Nice to meet you," Brash said.

The girls stammered somewhat over their greeting, all their eyes involuntarily straying to Brash's bare chest. Maddy bit back a smile at their reaction as she stood and tossed her husband his shirt. It seemed that all women reacted to him that way, especially after a photo of him had circulated around social media. Even the newspaper had included it alongside the article about Nigel Barret's untimely death at their wedding reception. The couple was forced to spend their honeymoon in seclusion at home, which was when a prying reporter had snapped the photo.

"The kids had a great time last night," Madison said to the girls, forcing them to pull their eyes away from her husband. "Thanks for including them. It's nice to put faces with the names."

"We had a lot of fun!" Rachel gushed. This time, her eyes strayed to Blake. She clearly had a crush on him. "Blake's a great volleyball player."

He scrambled to his feet with a new surge of energy. "Baseball is where I really shine." Modesty was not his strong suit.

"Really? I love baseball!"

"Too bad it's not a thing down here on the beach."

"But there's football. The guys said something about tossing the ball around later." She twirled her dark hair around her finger. "Wanna come when they get back from fishing?"

"Sure!"

"Y'all should come, too," Lindsey said to his sisters. "It'll be fun."

Patty remained silent. Madison noticed the way the girl's eyes darted toward the dunes. She looked a bit nervous, leaving Madison to wonder if the man from last night had spooked her, as well. Was he out there now, watching?

"Hey, wanna walk with us? We're not going far," Lindsey said.

Bethani glanced at their parents for

permission.

"Y'all go ahead," Brash said. "Have fun with your friends. Just don't pick on Blake too much," he teased. "He's definitely outnumbered."

"Ah," Blake bemoaned theatrically. "Such a plight to bear." He stepped between Rachel and Lindsey and looped his arms through theirs. "Come on, Patty. Let's take a stroll."

"What about us?" his twin complained.

"You can come, too," he offered generously.

Patty lingered, her eyes now searching the people gathered on the beach.

"Patty?" Blake asked. "You coming, or what?"

"Yeah," the girl said. "Yeah, I'm coming." Her smile looking forced as she caught up with the others.

As Brash settled into the chair beside her, Madison asked, "Did you find that odd?"

"Find what odd?"

"The way Patty acted just now. She seemed to be looking for someone."

"Maybe there's some guy she hoped to see."

Madison shook her head. "No, that's not it. She looked nervous. Almost scared."

Brash turned around to scan their surroundings. "I don't see anyone who looks suspicious."

"Maybe he's hiding, like he was last night."

Brash was about to brush off her concerns when he spotted someone. "There, behind us. Is that Smith?"

"Where?"

"Walking there against the dunes. He just bent down."

"The guy in the blue long sleeves? That could be him. He has on a hat with a floppy brim, like you suggested."

"He acts like he's looking for seashells, but his head is up. He's watching the kids."

Worried, Madison said in a rush, "We shouldn't have let them go. Maybe I should call and tell them to come back."

"It's broad daylight. I don't think he's going to do anything. Let's just keep an eye out."

"The kids won't like it if they see us following them. That is what you're suggesting, right?"

"Let's just hang tight for a minute. I could be wrong. That guy might not be Smith, and he might really be looking for shells."

"Do you really believe that?" A touch of scorn slipped into her voice.

"All I'm saying is that we shouldn't overreact."

"Spoken like my level-headed husband," she mumbled beneath her breath.

"What do you want me to do? Barge down there and demand to see the shells he's collected? Harass him for being on the beach, same as us?"

"Of course not. But you could do…something."

"I am. I plan to keep an eye on him. Not just here, but back at the inn, too."

"Fine," Madison huffed. "By the way, did Vina find out anything on the car?"

"Only what we expected. The rental company can't divulge that sort of information. All they could confirm was that it was picked up in Mesquite." Brash stood from his chair. He made a show of stretching his back and swiveling at the waist, but he was actually trying to get a better vantage point of the man in the floppy-brimmed hat.

"We knew it would be a dead end," Madison said, "but it was worth a try. I'll call Derron and see if he can come up with anything. But Bob Smith is a very common, if not generic, name. I wonder where..."

Brash was too distracted to listen. Bob Smith had picked up his pace and was now out of sight.

"Why don't you stay here and watch our stuff?" he said abruptly, breaking into her rambling speech. "I think I'll go look for seashells."

"Really? You're just going to leave me here while you go off chasing this guy?"

"Someone needs to watch our stuff. The golf cart's a rental, you know."

"We'll take the key."

"Which probably fits half the carts on this beach. Please, babe. Just indulge me."

"Fine," she grumbled. "Just remember to keep your shirt on, so you don't call too much attention to yourself."

"What's that supposed to mean?"

"You know exactly what that's supposed to mean! If you go around without your shirt on, all eyes will be on you. No one would even notice a man in a long winter coat and hat!"

"Which he is no longer wearing. Which makes him easier to blend in with the crowd, and which therefore makes it harder for me to keep an eye on."

"You were the one to be so helpful," she reminded him.

"Guilty as charged," Brash agreed. "*Now* can my shirt and I go catch up with this guy?"

"Sure. Fine. Just go." Madison waved him away in irritation. "I'll sit here and bake in the sun."

He gave her a maddening smile as he dropped a kiss on the top of her head. "Then sit under the canopy."

Still grumbling under her breath, Madison dialed her phone.

"*In a Pinch Professional Services.*"

"Hey, Derron."

"Dollface!" her employee greeted her with true affection. "How's the beach?"

"Gorgeous."

"Send pictures to all us peons back here slaving at the office."

"All one of you?" she teased.

"At least I'm here working while you're there lounging in the sun. That's where you are, am I right? Because I can hear the roar of the ocean."

"Yep, sure am," she said, not the least bit sorry.

"Rub it in, why don't you?" Derron grumbled.

"I'm calling so that you can earn your paycheck, for once. I need you to do some snooping for me."

"I resent the *for once* comment, but I'm intrigued by the snooping comment."

"This may be a tough one. I need you to look up a guy named Bob Smith."

"You're kidding, right? That's like looking up John Doe."

"I know."

"Can you narrow it down? Hometown? Family? Known associates?"

Madison winced. "All I can tell you is that he's driving a rental, is forty-five-ish, and he has scars on his face, neck, and hands."

"Oh, well, in *that* case, I have plenty of information to go on," Derron said with heavy sarcasm.

"I know it's not much. Vina ran the license plate, and it belonged to a car rental, but of course they couldn't divulge any personal information. All she knew was that he picked it up in Mesquite."

"And *why* are we looking up this man?"

"Because he keeps showing up, and there's something very suspicious about him. The first couple of times we saw him, he was dressed in a winter coat with a hat pulled low over his face. He stuck out like a sore thumb. At least now he's dressed more subtly, but he's staying at the inn where we are, and he's very reclusive. Except we just spotted him down here on the beach, and he appears to be following our kids and some new friends they met."

"You don't by chance have a picture of him?"

"Sorry, but no."

"You're not giving me much to work with, you know," Derron complained.

"I know that. And you probably won't be able to find anything. But it's worth a try."

He blew out a heavy breath. "I'll let you know if I manage to find a needle in the proverbial haystack."

"Thanks, Derron."

"Just remember," he warned before hanging up the phone. "You owe me."

Madison took her husband's advice and moved under the shade of the canopy. She took a moment to check in with her best friend Genny and to see how her 'nieces' were doing. She smiled when Genny sent back pictures of the two. Just a few months old, and already they were beauties.

She sat back and finally relaxed, resting her head against the back of the chair. She found herself growing drowsy but was jarred awake when she heard Brash's voice.

"Give the kids a call, why don't you?" he suggested. He had a worried look on his face. "Tell them we've had a change in plans."

"Okay," Madison said, sensing his urgency. "Why? What's happened?"

"This Mr. Smith may be following the kids," her husband said, "but there's also someone following Mr. Smith. And he was smoking a cigarette."

The teens grumbled about leaving their friends, even though the three girls walked back with them. With promises of seeing them later, they waved goodbye before turning to their parents with a sulk.

"What was that for?" Bethani wanted to know. "Why did you make us come back so soon?"

"We need to talk to you," Madison said. "About tonight..."

"What about it?" Megan asked, sensing trouble.

"I'm not sure it's a good idea if you play football with your new friends tonight."

"Why not? We already told them we would be there!" Bethani protested.

"I know, but we've given it more thought, and we think it would be better if you stayed at the inn."

Blake frowned. "Why? What's wrong with our friends? You didn't like them?"

"It's not that. They seemed very nice," Madison assured him.

"Dad? You agree with Mama Maddy?" Megan asked.

"I do."

"Just tell us why!" Bethani insisted on a reason. "Why can't we hang out with them?"

Madison glanced at Brash, trying to decide how much to tell them. When he gave her a slight nod of approval, she asked, "Did any of you happen to notice Patty seemed a bit nervous?"

"Actually," Megan answered with a reluctant frown, "I did. She was very distracted. She couldn't keep up with the conversation and a couple of times, like when we first left, she fell behind. We had to wait on her at least twice to catch up with us."

"Yeah, I noticed that, too. She kept watching the people around us, like she was looking for someone," Bethani agreed.

"Has she said anything to any of you about someone bothering her?" Brash wanted to know.

"Bothering her? Like, how?" Blake asked.

"Like following her. Harassing her."

"Patty? She's like the nicest girl I've ever met. Why would someone want to harass her?"

"I hoped you could tell us."

"She didn't say anything to me," Bethani said.

"Me, either," Megan agreed.

"Or me. I admit she's quieter than the others and looks a little sad, but I can't imagine why anyone would ever want to harass her," Blake said.

"What aren't you telling us?" Megan asked her father.

"Maybe it's nothing. Maybe it has nothing to do with Patty. But we noticed how nervous she seemed earlier. And we also noticed," he paused for a beat, taking a breath, "that someone seemed to be following you on your walk."

"What do you mean, following us?" Bethani squeaked.

"Was it that creepy guy from last night?" Megan asked.

"I don't think so. I think it was the man with the long coat. But he's wearing different clothes now. And he's staying at the inn."

Bethani jumped when she heard the news. "What? That's even more creepy!"

Megan looked wary. "You don't think the guy in the coat and the pervert from last night are the same person?"

"No. Because I saw that guy, too. It looked like he was following the first one."

"I hate to tell you this, Daddy D," Blake said, slapping his hand on his father's shoulder. "Looks like we may have a mystery on our hands this week, after all."

9

In light of the latest situation, the game of football was changed to a small gathering at the inn. Normally, Sirenity didn't allow parties, but she made an exception for them. The innkeeper offered them use of the fire pit and picnic table, happy to host them as long as they didn't play their music too loud or become too rowdy.

While the kids played corn hole and horseshoes and enjoyed another evening around a fire, Madison and Brash sat on the overhead balcony. They weren't spying on the party. They watched for anyone lurking in the shadows.

"I'm not seeing anything," Madison admitted. "Are you?"

"No, but there's a glare from the fire. I can't see that side of the property very well. I think I'll go down and wander around. See if I spot anything."

"Please be careful."

"Always, babe," Brash assured her.

Sirenity wandered out to the balcony after he had gone.

"Looks like the kids are having fun."

Madison smiled. "Thanks again for letting them invite their friends over." She motioned to the chair. "Have a seat."

Sliding into the chair, Sirenity told her, "I enjoy having young people here. And since there are only a few other guests at the inn, I don't see any harm in it."

"None of the others complained? I was worried about that."

"The Klintworths took their little boys to the Pleasure Pier in Galveston. See that red light way over there? That's the Ferris wheel. On a clear night like tonight, you can see it and some of the other buildings."

"What about the other couple, the ones celebrating their anniversary? A bunch of teenagers doesn't cramp their style?" Madison smiled, remembering how she and Gray had been when they were young and first married.

"Has it cramped yours and Brash's?" Sirenity's blue eyes twinkled. "Aren't you here celebrating yours, too?"

"Yes, but three of those teenagers down there are ours," Madison pointed out. "It's different for young couples."

The frown appeared again across Sirenity's forehead; the same one she had the last time she mentioned the couple. "When they called and booked the room, I had the distinct feeling they were here to... seek my help. But I don't get that vibe in person. They seem a little stand-offish."

"About that. I owe you an apology about last

night," Madison told her.

"How's that?"

"I guess my analytical mind has trouble processing abstract theories. I should have been more open-minded."

"That's okay. My abstract mind has trouble processing analytical reasoning." Sirenity laughed.

"Aren't we the pair?" Madison returned with a smile.

"I think it's important to be open to a variety of possibilities and thought processes."

"Which I wasn't. And I do apologize. Which leads me to my next question. What other vibes do you get from Mr. Smith? Do you think it's possible he could be dangerous?"

"No, I honestly don't. I saw him out here on the deck while you and Brash were down there talking to the kids. He looked… exceedingly sad, but at the same time, he had a smile on his face."

"Hmm. That's interesting."

"Look. I don't do any of your fancy investigating. I act purely on instinct. And my instinct tells me that, if anything, Mr. Smith just wants to protect them."

"One of those girls," Madison said carefully, conscious of how much she shared, "seems very nervous. Like she's waiting for something bad to happen."

Sirenity's brow creased in concern. "Which one?"

"The sandy-haired girl with braids. Her name is Patty. She's here at the beach with her roommate's family."

Sirenity studied the girl below. "She looks rather sad, doesn't she? She may be smiling, but it looks a bit forced."

"I know you don't like invading your guests' privacy, but can you tell me anything about this Mr. Smith? Do you know where he's from? Anything personal about him, other than that he looks sad?"

"I really shouldn't…"

"Please, Sirenity. This is important. There's something strange going on, and somehow my kids and their new friends are tangled up in it. I need to know if this man poses a danger."

"Strange? Like what?"

"I can't offer you specifics right now," Madison said, unwilling to lay blame without being certain. "But please trust me on this."

After a long moment, Sirenity relented. "He gave me an address about as generic as the name Bob Smith. PO Box 321, Austin, Texas."

"But he picked up his rental near Dallas. That doesn't make sense," Madison objected. "And, dressed like he was when he arrived, we thought he was from up north somewhere."

"I suspect the address isn't real, but the credit card accepted it and went through."

"Major label?"

"No, one of those generic brands. Probably the kind meant to boost your credit score."

"Or to hide your true identity," Madison murmured.

"Scary thought, but yeah. That's always a

possibility."

"He hasn't told you *anything* about himself?"

"Other than the fact that he prefers to be left alone and to eat in his room? Nothing."

Madison mulled over her thoughts, trying to make sense of it all.

"If you had to guess, what do you think his scars are from? Glass? Fire? A surgery gone bad?"

"It's hard to say, but my guess is none of the above." She shifted in her seat before continuing, "About sixteen or seventeen years ago, there was a terrible explosion at one of the nearby oil refineries. It killed dozens of people. Most of those who did survive were left with scars and majors burns over their bodies. Some were maimed for life. If I were to guess, I would say his scars resemble chemical burns, the kind so many people suffered after that explosion."

"That sounds awful. Did they find the cause of the explosion?"

"There was a rumor that one of their top chemists warned of impending disaster. He supposedly begged them to reevaluate their formulas and adjust some of their protocols, but the higher ups ignored him. Again, it was rumor and speculation, and of course, the execs denied everything. They blamed it on faulty equipment. But Mr. Smith's scars do remind me of the ones people suffered from the explosion and the subsequent fire that broke out."

"I remember seeing an article about that in your dining room. It sounded terrible."

"It was, especially if it could have been avoided."

"You think I could find out more about it on the internet?"

"I know you can. The company's high-priced lawyers have been fighting off lawsuits for years, but it's finally going to court. It's stirred up a lot of attention again."

"Okay, thanks. I'll check that out."

Sirenity peeked over the railing for another view of the party. "Would you excuse me for a few moments? I should go down and make sure there's still plenty of ice for their soft drinks."

"Do you need help? After all, my kids are the one who invited the others over."

"You just stay here and relax. I've got this."

Madison suspected it was more than just a simple ice refill, but she wasn't going to call her friend on it. At this point, if it kept those young people down there safe, she would entertain even the most abstract of ideas.

A good half hour later, Sirenity returned, carrying two glasses of wine.

"I hope you weren't icing down wine for the kids," Madison teased.

"Not at all. I even went so far as to check labels on all the cans. Soft drinks, only."

"That's good. At least they're showing signs of using good judgment." She took a sip of the wine and let it slide down her throat. "Hmm, so good. By the way, did you see Brash while you were down there?"

"No. But to be honest, I wasn't really looking

for him. I was talking to Patty."

Madison smiled. "Why am I not surprised?"

Getting straight to the point, Sirenity said, "Conversation-wise, I found out that Patty lives with her divorced mother in Lufkin. She's leaning toward pursuing a career in pharmaceuticals. It's never been my cup of tea, personally, but she loves science and all things chemistry." A slight shudder rocked through her shoulders, eliciting a chuckle from her friend.

"For the record, I feel the same way," Madison broke in, mimicking the shudder.

"She seems like a very intelligent, conscientious young woman. She has excellent manners, and I think she has a solid head on her shoulders. She doesn't strike me as someone who takes unnecessary chances."

"You said conversation-wise?"

"Yes. She offered to help with the ice, so we had a nice little talk."

Madison nodded. "Now tell me what you learned from your non-conversation."

"You're sure?" Sirenity asked.

"I told you; I do apologize for doubting you last night. Admittedly, I'm still on the fence about this whole vibe-reading concept, but I'm willing to listen with an open mind."

"Fair enough. Patty strikes me as being very sad. She and her mom apparently had a hard time of it, with little to no support from her father. She doesn't even know if he's still alive. But I got the distinct feeling she's afraid of something, or of someone. My guess is she came to the beach with her friend to get away from whatever, or whoever, is troubling her."

"An over-controlling mother? It could be that her mother's having trouble with her growing up, since it's just been the two of them all these years."

"Maybe."

"But you don't think so."

Sirenity shook her head. "This feels… darker… than that. I think she's being stalked."

A slight gasp escaped Madison. How had Sirenity known that? "Did she—Did she tell you that?"

"No. It's just the feeling I discerned," Sirenity admitted. "I think she believed coming here with friends would throw her stalker off, but now she's afraid he followed her."

Madison bit her lip. She hadn't shared any details with her friend about Bob Smith following the kids, or about the other man following Bob Smith. Without being privy to this information, Sirenity was eerily on target with her assessment.

Madison was curious as to what else the innkeeper had discerned. "A crazy ex-boyfriend, you think?"

"Maybe. It's hard to say."

Madison looked down at the group, all of them laughing and having a good time. It broke her heart that Patty didn't feel as light and carefree as her friends. At that age, all she should have to worry about was making good grades, good friends, and memories that would last a lifetime.

Nibbling on her lip, Madison said, "Sadly, I think she may be right."

Brash circled around the perimeter of the property, staying well within the shadows. If anyone else was out here, he wanted to be behind them.

He found a place he could stop and observe, watching for signs of movement or the hint of a cigarette. He found neither.

On his second round, he saw him. It wasn't the unknown stalker. It was Mr. Smith.

"Nice evening, isn't it?" Brash said, opting for the friendly approach. "Good night for a stroll."

With a jolt, the other man jerked around to see who spoke.

"Yeah," he agreed. His voice sounded rough.

"I see you took my advice and bought some of those fishing shirts with UV protection. I wear a lot of those, myself."

"Uh, yeah. Yeah. Thanks." The man turned away, obviously hoping to end the unwanted conversation.

"I didn't introduce myself the other day. Brash deCordova."

The man looked skeptical about the hand Brash offered, but he cautiously accepted the handshake. "Bob. Bob Smith."

Not waiting for an invitation, Brash took a spot beside Bob Smith. They stood just outside the circle of light cast from the fire.

"Looks like they're having a good time, doesn't

it?" Brash kept his voice conversational as he nodded toward the young people. "I remember days like that, don't you? Not a care in the world, except to have fun."

"I guess," Smith muttered.

"You have any kids, Bob Smith?"

"What's it to you?" Smith asked harshly. "Why do you ask?"

Curious about his reaction, Brash hid it behind a causal shrug. "Just making conversation."

"I came out here for some peace and quiet, not for conversation," Smith answered gruffly.

Brash held up his hands in a gesture of peace. "Just trying to be friendly," he told him. "That, and to check on my kids." He nodded to the young people gathered around the fire. "Three of those are mine, by the way."

Smith looked uncomfortable, shifting slightly in his new clothes.

"And I will do anything to protect them," Brash said in a voice meant to demand respect. His eyes bore into Smith, until the other man felt compelled to meet his gaze. Staring him straight in the eyes, Brash's tone was a warning within itself. "I don't know who you are, Bob Smith, and I don't know what you're up to. But I'll find out. And if you do one thing to harm any one of them—" he pointed to the group at the fire pit "—my kids, or someone else's, I will hunt you down, and I will make you pay. Are we clear on that?"

"We're clear," Smith answered shortly. "And for the record, it's not me who wants to cause harm."

Brash studied him for a moment, trying to gauge his sincerity. He detected a hint of fear in the man, and he didn't think it came from the threat he had just issued. This was something else.

"Then you must be referring to the man following you."

A look of panic filled Smith's face. "There's someone following me?"

"You didn't know?"

"What? No!" Bob Smith ran his hand over his shaggy dirty-blond hair, knocking his hat off in the process. He bent to retrieve it, an agonized expression on his scarred face. "This wasn't supposed to happen! I thought I was being so careful."

"What's going on, Smith? Maybe I can help you."

"No. No, the less people involved, the better."

"Smith," Brash reminded him in a stern voice, "three of those are my kids out there."

"He's not after them. It's me he's after."

"Why?"

"That's not important."

"That's where you're wrong. I followed you today while you were tagging along after my kids and their new friends. And I don't think it's the first time. Were you there last night when they were playing volleyball in the sand?"

Smith hesitated before answering, "And if I was? What's the harm in watching a group of young people having fun?"

"Because he was there, too. He's been

following you. To the volleyball game. To the inn. He was following you today, the same way I did. And you've led him straight to those kids. Which means you've involved my kids in this now. So, yes, Bob Smith, this *is* my business," Brash told him in a voice hard as steel. "I need to know what's going on, why those men are after you, and how I can protect my family."

"Just keep your kids away from the others."

"Not good enough."

"It will have to be, because that's all I'm saying." His voice hardened with determination. "I don't know who you are, either, so butt out of this."

"I'm trying to be an ally. I'm trying to help."

"Just keep your kids away," Smith said brusquely. The more he talked, the hoarser his voice became. "That's help enough."

When Smith brushed past him and blended deeper into the shadows, Brash didn't try to stop him.

After the party was over, the mess cleared away, and the kids were off to their rooms, Madison and Brash shared notes on this evening's revelations.

"I know you said absolutely no snooping this week," Madison began, ready to present a strong argument to her husband. "But I think this changes everything, don't you?" she asked, pacing their bedroom.

"Yes, I do."

"Wait. What?" She whirled around, taken by surprise when he agreed.

"I agree. This changes things."

"Are you saying what I think you're saying?"

Brash made a flourishing movement with his hand. "Yes. By all means, snoop to your heart's content." Before she could fly across the room and into his arms, he added one very critical condition. "As long as," he clarified, "your snooping is contained to an internet search. I'll do any legwork required."

"That's not fair!" she protested.

"I give you my full blessing to dig around in every virtual file you can find. But I will not put you in danger. This is non-negotiable, Madison. Snoop virtually, or not it all."

"But what about you? You could be in danger, too, you know!" she protested.

"I'm a trained professional. There is a difference."

"Not to a criminal, there's not."

"Look. I'm not going to do anything tonight. Blake and I have to be out on the water early in the morning. While we're gone, do your thing on the internet. We'll reassess when I get back. Fair enough?"

Madison huffed out a sigh. "Would it do any good if I said no, I don't think that's at all fair?"

"None at all."

10

THE SISTERS

It was Virgie's turn to sit with Ella Getty.

Granny Bert didn't tell her old friend about Ella's claims the day before. She wanted to see if the woman was still telling the same story today. She might make some even wilder statement to Virgie. The friends could compare notes at the end of the day.

"Ella? It's Virgie. Do you remember me from yesterday?"

"Of course I remember you. You brought me breakfast."

"Yes, that's right. What about today? Have you already eaten, or can I make you something?"

"Yes, and yes. Banisha fed me some glob she called oatmeal, but that girl never was much of a cook. She certainly didn't take after me and Gracie," Ella sniffed.

"It doesn't sound like it," Virgie agreed amicably. "What would you like? Eggs? Toast?"

"Yes, and yes," the other woman repeated. "Fried, if you please."

"Certainly. Coming right up."

With the eggs and toast ready to serve, Virgie asked Ella where she would like to eat.

"Kitchen table is fine."

Virgie had a cup of coffee while her companion ate. When Ella noticed, she looked down at her plate in suspicion. "You're not eating? Why? Did you put something in here?"

"Of course not. But I ate at home when I made breakfast for Hank."

"Who's Hank?"

"My husband."

"If you're married, why are you over here?"

"Because Banisha asked me to come. She asked all of us, really, so we'll take turns visiting with you. Doesn't that sound nice?"

The other woman grunted. "If you say so."

"Do you have other children, besides Banisha?"

"I gave birth to six. All three boys died, either at birth or in the Army. That just leaves the girls. Banisha is the oldest, so she got stuck with me."

"Don't talk like that. I'm sure the other girls would take you if they could."

"That's not what Prancy says. Ten hours of labor, and that's the gratitude I get."

"Where do your daughters live?"

"Prancy lives over in Houston County. Less than two hours away and still doesn't have time to visit her old mammy. Tulsa lives in Houston, the city.

Opposite direction, same distance. She doesn't come much, either."

"It's easy to get caught up in life," Virgie agreed on a sigh, "and forget to take time for family."

"No one respects their elders anymore," Ella complained. "Did I treat my parents that way? No, ma'am, I did not!" she said emphatically. "My momma would have tanned my hide, if she had lived that long. 'Course, after what happened to sweet Gracie, I reckon it's a good thing she passed so young. It would have broke her heart, worse than it broke my pappy's."

"What happened to Gracie?"

Ella's face shut down. "I told you yesterday," she snapped. "I don't talk about the past. And that's that!" She brushed her hands together briskly and pushed away her empty plate. "I'm going to watch my shows now. Don't bother me."

Virgie wisely kept her mouth shut, wondering what had just happened.

After her morning game shows and a long nap, Ella was in a better mood. She told Virgie a tale about a romance she had in one of the nursing homes she lived in. She said she and Ralph started as partners in forty-two, but soon became much more. They liked to sneak out and meet under the tree in the courtyard. She said when the night nurse caught them, someone chopped down the tree and made firewood out of it. The next time they were caught together, they both had to wear bracelets that lit up like fireworks when they ventured outside without 'proper supervision.' The third time was the real clencher. They were simply taking a shower together, but *some* people didn't approve of such, she said with a huff. Ella had to move after that. She heard that Ralph died shortly afterwards, surely of a broken heart.

Virgie didn't know if any of it was true, but Ella enjoyed telling it. She followed it with a story of sneaking aboard a freight train one time and riding it all the way to Hearne, where they had relatives.

That story Virgie believed. She and her brother had tried doing the same thing once but weren't as successful. Their adventure had ended with a visit to the woodshed and extra chores for a week.

"My pappy was spittin' mad!" Ella recalled. "He made me stay there for three days before he paid a neighbor to drive over and fetch me home. Then he told me I had to work for Mr. Jenkins—that was our neighbor—to pay for his time and trouble. After that, I didn't much fancy a train ride anymore."

"I imagine not!" Virgie chuckled along with her.

"Course, I did take one more train ride." A coy smile played around her lips. "With Ernest."

"Ernest?"

"I never told you about Ernest?" she asked, acting as if the two of them were old friends. "Law, girl," she drawled, using the old Southern slang for lord. "Pull your chair up close and let me tell you all about Ernest."

This tale was racy and too outlandish to be true, but Virgie listened all the same. She supposed this was what Banisha had meant by not believing a thing her mother told them, but her stories were innocent enough. Maybe *innocent* wasn't the right word, Virgie corrected herself, not if Ella's stories of Ernest and showering with Ralph were true. But they were harmless. Just an old woman's fantasies that lived in her head. A way of whiling her hours away when her children were too busy for her.

By early afternoon, Virgie thought this assignment wasn't nearly as hard as Banisha had made it sound. Her mother was just lonely.

That was before Ella asked to sit on the back porch. After that, everything changed.

"Pappy had his garden out yonder," she said, pointing with an arthritic finger. "He grew squash, zucchini, peas, taters, onions. You name it, he could grow it."

"Corn?"

"Stalks as high as his head," Ella boasted. "So thick and tall, it was easy for a body to get lost in among them." Her smile faltered then, and a shadow moved behind her eyes. "Something happened out there..." she murmured. "I don't rightly recall what it was now, but something we didn't talk about. Something evil."

Her eyes drifted to the big pin oak near the edge of the fence. "Evil," she whispered. "Evil, like that tree."

"Trees aren't evil, Ella. They're one of God's mightiest creations. Just look at how tall and straight it is, with big shady leaves and—"

"I said it was evil!" Ella snapped. "Don't sass

me, young lady."

"I don't know about the young part. Fact is, I'm not sure which one of us is older, you or me."

"I didn't ask your age. I asked you what you did with the shovel."

Virgie frowned. "What shovel?"

"The one you used to dig the hole!"

"What hole?"

"You have trouble hearing, girl? Or just trouble following directions? I told you to hide that shovel and to never speak of this again. Never."

It took a moment for Virgie to catch on, but Ella was reliving a memory. Or what she *thought* was a memory. It could easily be another figment of her imagination. Her voice came out an octave lower than normal, like she was trying to mimic a man's voice. Her father's, perhaps? Had she once gotten in trouble for digging a hole in his garden?

"You're right," Virgie went along, hoping to appease her. "I'm sorry."

Ella grunted. After a long while, she shook her head and tried to smile. "That old nurse said she chopped it down, but she was just foolin' us. There it stands, as tall as can be."

She was back to her Ralph fantasy. She hopped subjects so fast it was hard to keep up.

"See? I told you. Trees aren't evil."

Another switch flipped. "They are! They are evil! Someone needs to cut that one down, too! Take me back inside. I don't want to look at it for another minute."

From there, the whole afternoon went downhill.

11

Madison got up well before daylight. She saw the guys off for the fishing trip and then pulled out her laptop. She had snooping to do.

Most of what Sirenity told her about the explosion at Tar-Go Chemical was there on the web. One of their refineries had suffered a horrific accident, resulting in numerous casualties and even more injuries. Supposedly, a whistle blower had warned of the impending danger, but officials chose to ignore him. Due to safety concerns and on-going litigation, that person's name was being withheld.

The almost two-decade-long saga was finally going to trial. A jury pool had been selected in Beaumont, and final motions were being presented to the court. Unless the case hit yet another snag, the trial was expected to start at the beginning of the month.

Madison pulled up dozens of old articles and on-scene footage of the chaotic aftermath from the explosion. Some were almost too graphic to watch. The injuries suffered were horrible. She could almost smell the putrid scent of toxic smoke through her computer screen.

"Too early in the morning for that," she murmured. She switched gears, deciding to look up everything she could find on Patty. "What did she tell me her last name was? Richards? Roberts? Yes, that right. Patty Roberts from Lufkin, Texas." She put the name in her search engine and let the internet do its magic.

Patricia "Patty" Roberts was an exemplary student. Valedictorian of her senior class. President of the Honor Society. Recipient of a full academic scholarship to Sam Houston State University. Daughter of Loretta Roberts, with no mention of a father. No siblings. Nothing the least bit scandalous in her past. She appeared to be just as she seemed in person—a hardworking, conscientious student who took her studies seriously.

"So why is someone stalking her?" Madison wondered aloud. "I don't see any social media presence for her. No obvious boyfriend lurking in her past. No disgruntled employer who accused her of stealing."

"So, maybe a fellow student, jealous of her success?" Madison further speculated. "Someone who thought they deserved the top honors instead of her. It's hard to imagine anything more than that. Patty is almost so clean she squeaks."

Madison considered another angle. What if it was because of her mother? Did Loretta Roberts have some dark secret she kept hidden? Was someone using Patty to get to her mother?

Nothing panned out on Loretta Roberts, nor any of Patty's former classmates that Madison could find. She soon abandoned those searches for one on Bob Smith, even though she knew how that would go. Derron hadn't gotten back with her, not even to complain about the futility of her request.

There were hundreds of Bob Smiths. Perhaps thousands. Too many to wade through, even when she narrowed the parameters of her search. She even put in keywords like *scars*, *chemical burns*, and, on a lark, *Tar-Go Chemical.*

Nothing.

Madison made another cup of coffee and kept searching.

Somewhere along the way, her searches mingled. She put in a wrong keyword and up popped a new slew of pages. Somehow, she was on the employee rosters of Tar-Go Chemical's upper management team and their top chemists.

Sirenity had mentioned it was a chemist who sounded the alarm on the incorrect method being used at the refinery. The explosion had taken place seventeen years ago. So even if the news refused to identify the person by name, the roster from that year might give her a better clue. She wasn't sure how it factored into things, but it was worth a try. She was out of better ideas for now.

It took another cup of coffee, a quick shower, and page after page of digging, but Madison finally found something of interest. One of the chemists at the refinery was Samuel Roberts.

Samuel Roberts. Bob Smith. Could they be one

in the same? The photo was old and not of the best quality. The man in the picture and the man in the long coat looked nothing alike, even though she had yet to see Mr. Smith's face clearly. He had kept most of it covered the few times she had seen him. But Sirenity might know, or Brash.

She downloaded the photo and transferred it to her phone.

The roster gave a brief recap of the chemist's degrees and qualifications for the job. Another search confirmed the information, but after the explosion, nothing else was on record for Samuel Roberts. The man had vanished.

Had he been killed in the explosion, and his body never identified? According to the various news articles, even after all these years, there were still two bodies without names. Was one of them the chemist? And if not, what had happened to him? How had he just fallen off the radar?

It was too much to contemplate on an empty stomach, especially with three cups of coffee in her system. She felt jittery and needed to eat. The girls were still sleeping, so Madison left a note and went down for a solo trip to the buffet.

As expected, Mr. Smith was nowhere to be seen. It was still early, so the only person she saw up and moving was the father of the young boys. He was outside on the deck with his coffee, meaning she had the dining room to herself.

"You look deep in thought," Sirenity said. She carried in a basket of muffins and placed them on the buffet, but not before offering one to Madison.

"Banana nut."

"Sure. If they're as good as your strawberry ones, I may take the entire basket."

Smiling, Sirenity noticed she was drinking only juice and water. "No coffee this morning?"

"I've already had three cups in my room. I'll pass for now."

Sirenity raised an eyebrow. "You must have gotten up early."

"I saw Brash and Blake off on their fishing trip and then did a little work on the computer."

"I thought you were officially off work this week. Vacation, remember?"

"This just came up."

Sirenity's thoughtful gaze roamed over her. "You're investigating Mr. Smith."

Madison squirmed in her seat. "Maybe."

"Why?"

"Come on, Sirenity, you know why. My curious mind, his reclusive behavior, now him practically stalking my kids... Of course I'm investigating him!"

"Stalking your kids? Isn't that a little bit of an exaggeration? Yes, he was watching the party, but—"

"It's more than that, Sirenity. I admit, his attention seems more focused on their friends, but he's been stalking their group. Following them. He was at their volleyball game night before last. He was following them on the beach. He was watching them last night. Not just from the deck, but down below, too. This involves my family, so, yes, I am researching him."

"Were we wrong about him being in the shadows the other night?"

"No. That was… someone else."

Sirenity looked alarmed. "There's someone else involved in this. Who? Are they staying here at the inn?"

"No. I'm not sure who this other man is, but he appears to be trailing Bob Smith. I think that was why he was watching the inn the other night."

Sirenity's eyes clouded with worry. "This is so much more than I thought," she murmured.

"I have something I want to show you." Madison pulled up the photo from the internet and showed it to her friend. "Do you recognize this man?"

After studying the picture, Sirenity shook her head. "The eyes look familiar, but I don't think I know him."

"Do you think there's any chance this could be Bob Smith? Twenty years ago, and without the scars?"

"Can I enlarge this?"

"Sure." Madison made the picture larger. "Is that better?"

"It helps." Tilting her dark head from one side to another, Sirenity perused the photo. Her finger hovered just above the screen, tracing the shape of his face to get a better sense of his identity. "The face structure is the same," she determined. "The eyes are close, although Mr. Smith's hold a deep sadness. The scarring makes the nose different, but maybe he had reconstructive surgery. I can't be certain, but I think there's a distinct possibility this could be my guest."

She handed the phone back to Madison. "Where did this picture come from?"

"I found it on the internet. This man, Samuel Roberts, was a chemist for Tar-Go Chemical."

"The company that owned the oil refinery."

"Exactly."

"And you think this Samuel Roberts is Bob Smith?"

Madison nodded. "I think it's possible."

Sirenity absorbed the information, running the possibilities and known facts through her head. "Patty is his daughter, isn't she?" she asked quietly.

Madison sat back, blinking in surprise. "Wow. I hadn't even considered that. How—How did you..."

"I listen, remember?" Sirenity smiled. "It fits. Bob Smith is here searching for something. He's trying to make amends for something he lost, something that was precious to him. Patty is a sad young woman without a father. I didn't understand the look on his face the other night when he was watching the kids from the railing, but his gaze was almost reverent. It fits."

"Wow," Madison repeated. She let it all sink in before nodding slowly. "You're right. It does. Did I mention her name is Patty Roberts?"

"See? It all makes sense."

"The question is, why is he here? And why is he being so secretive?"

"He was a chemist, right? Could he be the whistle blower?"

"After the explosion, I couldn't find anything

else on Samuel Roberts. They never identified the whistle blower by name, but they still have two unidentified bodies. I think Roberts either died in the accident or was the whistle blower. He must have changed his name and fallen off the radar."

"My guess is the latter," Sirenity said. "I think he probably kept tabs on Patty all these years, and he finally has a chance to meet her, or at least to see her."

"But she probably doesn't even know who he is."

"But her mother does," Sirenity pointed out. "She might not want him anywhere near their daughter."

"You're right. He hasn't been in Patty's life all these years, so why disrupt it now? She's trying to protect her daughter."

"But she's here with friends this week, so this is his chance." Sirenity glanced at her watch. "I'm sorry to cut this short, but I need to get back to the kitchen. I have baked oatmeal in the oven."

"Oops, sorry. I didn't mean to keep you from your work."

"I'm glad you shared this with me. It explains so much, and yet it still leaves so many questions. Mainly, what is it that he needs from me? How can I help him?"

"Maybe you already did," Madison suggested. "Last night, when Patty came to the inn, he was able to watch her from the deck. It's probably the best vantage point he's ever had, and he could watch her without being conspicuous."

"It's a thought," Sirenity agreed. The alarm went off on her phone. "We'll talk later, okay?"

"Sure. Go." Madison waved her off. "Don't let me stop you from doing your thing with another fabulous buffet. I'll just help myself to another muffin..."

Sirenity kept breakfast out later than normal, waiting for Brash and Blake to return. Brash was lucky to fill his plate before Blake ate everything that was left. Madison joined them in the dining room to be regaled by stories of their adventure.

"It was great, Mom!" Blake said enthusiastically, stuffing the last muffin in his mouth. "I'm seriously rethinking my career goals. I'm thinking of becoming a fishing guide now. Do you know how much money I could rake in every year, just by doing something I love?"

Amused by his excitement, she chuckled. "Professional baseball player. Famous actor. Owning a game ranch. Now professional fishing guide. My, my, what a busy man you'll be."

Blake considered her words as he ate another sausage. "I may have to let the acting gig go," he agreed. "But I could probably juggle the rest. Hire someone to run the game ranch for me, play pro ball, and in the off season, run the guide business."

"But I thought you wanted to guide hunts on your massive game ranch."

"I figure that will take a nice hunk of cash, which I could easily earn with both careers. The game ranch could be my backup when my pitching arm wears out."

Brash, too, was amused. "At least he's thinking ahead and has a back-up plan."

"So," Madison asked, "where are all those fish I see in the photos?"

"We didn't know how Sirenity felt about a fish fry here at the inn, so Kent is doing it at his place. Tonight," he added. "I hope that's okay?"

"It's a little late to ask that, don't you think?" Madison laughed. "But we don't have any other dinner plans, so it's fine."

Blake answered, but his eyes were on the buffet. "Cool. I see some fruit up there, so I think I'll snag it before Sirenity takes it away. Be right back."

"Where does that boy put it all?" she marveled, not for the first time.

"That's really why you married me, wasn't it?" Brash teased. "You couldn't afford the grocery bill, so you decided to let me foot the bill."

"That, and because I couldn't live without you."

"Buttering me up, are you? I can tell by that look on your face that you did your snooping this morning, and you can't wait to tell me what you found."

"You're right. I have a theory." She lowered her voice. "But I don't want to get into it here. You know how you said that young couple was listening to your conversation with Mr. Smith the other day? I think they're listening to ours, too. So, hurry up and eat, so we can go to the room, and I can show you what I found."

His dark eyes glittered. "You had me at 'go to the room.' You lost me at the real reason."

Madison wrinkled her nose. "The other real reason is that you smell like a fish, and the kids are here."

"See? There can be benefits to an empty nest."

She put a hand up to stop him. "Do not say those words to me. I can't think about an empty nest right now—maybe not ever, to be honest—but right now, my head is about to explode with what I've found."

"Then I'd better finish my breakfast. Especially before Blake sees I have eggs left and decides to polish them off for me."

12

The moment Brash stepped from the shower and into the living room of their suite, Madison proceeded with her news.

"I have a theory."

"So you said downstairs." He settled onto the couch beside her. "Let's hear it."

"I did so much digging that I started to go cross-eyed. I looked up Patty, trying to find what it is that frightens her so much. She came back squeaky clean. The girl's not even on social media. So, I looked up her mother. Loretta Roberts' information was boring, at best. No juicy past there. And Bob Smith was a total bust. Literally a ton of hits, but no way of finding the one I wanted.

"I also looked up Tar-Go Chemicals and the explosion that took place at their oil refinery almost twenty years ago. Sirenity told me that Mr. Smith's scars reminded her of the scars many of the burn victims had. Anyway, I was getting tired, and I somehow got my searches all mixed up. But my mistake paid off big time because I think I found Mr.

Bob Smith."

"Really?" He sounded surprised.

A note of uncertainty slipped into her voice. ""I think. Here. Look at this picture. Do you think this could be our mysterious Mr. Smith when he was younger? And before he had scars on his face?"

Brash looked at her phone. "Maybe," he said, but he sounded doubtful. "It's hard to tell. Explain why you think it's him."

"The man in the picture is a chemist by the name of Samuel Roberts. His nickname was Smitty."

Brash mulled over the names. "Smitty Roberts. Bob Smith." He shrugged. "I suppose it's possible. But surely, you have more than this."

"I do. According to Sirenity and the various news articles I've found, a top chemist blew the whistle on unsafe protocols at the refinery, but Tar-Go execs ignored his warnings. Not long after that, the explosion happened. His name was never released, partly for his own protection and partly because there was ongoing litigation. In fact, it's been seventeen years since the accident, and the case is just now going to trial. It's set to start at the beginning of April. Anyway, after the explosion, Samuel Roberts completely fell off the radar. I can't find anything on him."

"Could he have been killed during the explosion? I'm sure something like that had causalities."

"Dozens of them. And yes, there are still two bodies that haven't been identified yet, so it's possible his is one of them. But it's also possible that he changed his name, especially if this picture looks like the man you know as Bob Smith."

"Let me look at that again." Brash examined the photo more closely. "He does favor Smith," he agreed. "I guess it's possible. Seventeen years will age a man. An accident like that would double the effects."

"For all I know, this photograph could have been taken years before the explosion. But Sirenity thought it could be him, and now you do, too. Given that, I think it's very likely that Bob Smith was the chemist who predicted the disaster."

"And his superiors ignored him."

"Exactly. Which would explain why he felt the need to change his name and go underground."

Brash grinned at her. "Listen to you, with the lingo and all."

She swatted at his arm. "I'm being serious here. I think Bob Smith and Samuel Roberts are one and the same."

"And you think Patty is his daughter."

Madison rolled her eyes. "Well, I didn't, until Sirenity pointed out the obvious. Now both of you are making me feel like a moron for missing it."

He touched her arm. "Don't be so hard on yourself. It's easy to be so focused on the forest, you don't see the trees."

She frowned at the analogy. "I thought it was the other way around. You don't see the forest for the trees."

"Sometimes. In this case, you were looking at the broader picture, not the fine details. Patty is a detail you overlooked."

"But it explains so much. It explains why he came here in the first place. He's been in hiding for all this time, then shows up at a very public beach during Spring Break. No wonder he was wearing a hat and coat! He didn't want to be recognized."

"I doubt Patty hardly remembers him, much less would recognize him."

"But like Sirenity said, her mother would. This might be his only chance to get close to his daughter without Loretta interfering."

"She's been away at college," Brash pointed out. "He had opportunity there."

"Which I'm sure he took. That's probably why Patty is so nervous. She knows someone was stalking her at Sam, and now he's followed her to Crystal Beach."

"Makes sense."

"What doesn't make sense is this second guy. Why is he following Bob Smith? How does he factor into it?"

"You said the trial was coming up, right?"

"Yes. Next month."

"It stands to reason that the former chemist would be the star witness for the prosecution. Meaning someone might want to silence Samuel Roberts, aka Bob Smith."

Madison drew a sharp intake of breath. "You mean like a hit man?"

"Rein it in there, Blake," he teased, recalling their son's prediction the first time they saw Smith. "Maybe nothing quite so dramatic. Maybe they don't want to kill him. Maybe they want to pay him off. Or at least to scare him into silence. Smith was definitely spooked when I told him someone was following him. He said he had been so careful. And he said something about it wasn't him that wanted to cause harm."

"So, you think this other man has been following Smith, and now he knows where the daughter is. And he can use Patty to keep the key witness from testifying."

"Unfortunately, it happens all the time. These corporations have deep pockets. Tar-Go is a universal brand. They won't be shy about protecting their name and their reputation."

"Or their bottom line," she muttered.

"Exactly. Which I think is what this is all about."

"What do we do? How do we protect Smith? More importantly, how do we protect Patty?"

Brash rubbed his jaw. "I could probably call in a few favors. Get a detail to sit on Smith. In fact, I'm surprised the prosecution doesn't have him in a safe house somewhere."

"Maybe they did. Maybe that's what this cloak and dagger has been all about. Maybe he's also hiding from the people trying to protect him, just so he has the chance to see and talk to his daughter."

"If that's the case, then his second guy could be trying to protect him, not harm him." Brash thought about it for a minute before discarding the idea. "No, I don't think that's it. He was genuinely afraid. Not for himself, but for Patty. This second guy is definitely bad news."

"Again, what can we do?"

"I'll start by calling Vina. She has access to files you don't. She can confirm whether or not we're right, and if we are, we can plan from there."

"That means we have to wait, right?"

"The dirty little secret they never show on television," he confided with a smile. "Half of a lawman's job is waiting. Like it or not, doing the research and getting every detail right can make or break a case."

"You know I'm not good at waiting."

Pulling her into his arms, his smile turned slow and sexy. "I may just have a few ideas on how to make waiting less painful."

"Do you, now?" she asked, slipping her arms around his neck.

He lowered his mouth to hers. "I do."

"Ew, you two!" Blake's voice interrupted. "Get a room."

"We have one, and you're in it. Get out!" Brash replied. He tossed a throw pillow in the general direction of Blake's voice without lifting his head.

"Technically, this is the common room. And, besides, this is serious."

"So is kissing my wife."

"For real, you guys. I need to talk to you."

With a deeply put-out sigh, Brash released his hold on Maddy and straightened on the sofa. "Yes, son? What it is? And before you ask, no, you can't buy a boat and become a fishing guide."

"That's not what I wanted to ask." He frowned

as a new thought occurred to him. "And I hadn't even thought about the boat angle. Hey, Mom, doesn't Grandmother Annette have a trust fund set up for me when I turn twenty-one? Maybe I could—"

"No, Blake!" his parents said in unison.

He put up his hands in a defensive gesture. "Okay, chill. It was just a thought."

"I suppose you interrupted us for a reason?" his mother asked.

"Besides the fact that I don't want to be a big brother? Yeah, I did." He pointed to the chair. "Do I have permission to sit?"

"Stop being so dramatic," Madison sighed. "How can we help you?"

"I have a problem."

"Yeah, we got that part."

"So, I guess I gave out some mixed signals last night. See, Rachel thought I was into her, but last night, I sorta hovered around Patty. It was more out of protectiveness than actual interest, but Rachel didn't see it that way. So now she's mad at both of us. And I think Patty may have gotten the wrong idea, too, which I realize isn't exactly a bad thing. She's pretty awesome, herself. So now I don't know what to do."

Blake rarely came to his mother for relationship advice, but a recent break with his girlfriend had left him feeling a bit vulnerable. He and Danni Jo had been on and off for over a year, but the arrival of a new boy at school had made the *off* seem permanent. Not wanting to mess this one up, she glanced at Brash for guidance.

"Before last night, were you into Rachel?" He used the teen terminology easily, as if he did it every day. That was part of what made him so good at his job. He could relate to just about anyone.

"Yeah, I guess. We have the most in common. And if I stayed in touch with any of them after this week, it would probably be her."

"Which was my next question. Do you think you'll ever see any of these girls again?"

"Probably not."

"Then why ruin a perfectly good Spring Break and an existing friendship between the girls for something that doesn't really matter? Make it clear you want to be friends with all three of them, no hook-ups, and just enjoy the week."

"Yeah," the boy said, nodding his head. "Why didn't I think of that? Thanks, Daddy D. Thanks, Mom. Y'all are the best!" Whistling a tune, he left the room as quickly as he had come.

"I don't get it," Madison said. "He has girls fighting over him at home all the time. Why is this time any different?"

Brash wiggled his brows. "Because these are *college* girls."

"Aah," she said in sudden understanding.

"Whole new ballgame. Especially since he just lost Danni Jo to an underclassman. He had his confidence shaken up a bit."

"With my son and his ego, I didn't think it was possible."

"Everyone hits patches of doubt, sweetheart."

"Even the great Brash deCordova?" she

teased.

"Even him. Especially when the woman he was crazy about kept putting him off." He gave her a reproachful look.

"Who dared do that to you?" Madison asked in mock outrage.

"The only woman I've ever been truly crazy about," he said. "And the one who finally came to her senses and agreed to marry me, before I lost every shred of my dignity. I was this close to groveling, you know," he said, holding his fingers a hair's breadth apart.

"You were not," she said, giving him a playful push.

"Was so."

"You are so full of it, Brash deCordova. Just like your son. I swear, sometimes I think you two are actually blood related."

"I couldn't think of a nicer compliment."

"Both of you think you are so charming," she accused, "but you're maddening. That's what you are. You're completely maddening!" She tossed the other pillow at him as she stood from the sofa.

He pulled her back down, rubbing the pillow on her head. "You forgot adorable."

Megan appeared in the doorway. "Ooh, pillow fight!" she squealed. "Beth, come out here. And bring pillows!"

13

THE SISTERS

"I'm afraid this little hellcat is going to be too much for our sweet Sybil to handle," Virgie confided to Granny Bert.

"You noticed that, too, did you?"

"How could I not? I can't decide if the woman is stricken with dementia, or the devil!"

"You didn't make the mistake of taking her outside to the back porch, did you?"

Virgie gasped. "You knew about that and didn't warn me?"

"I wanted to see if it was a one-time lark, or if she'd tell you the same tale. Was the big pin oak evil?"

"Yes, and it should be chopped down, according to her."

"Did she happen to say why?" Granny Bert asked.

"No. But there was one really strange moment when she seemed to be talking in another person's voice. Like she was possessed. She asked me where the shovel was that I used to dig the hole. Told me not to sass her, to hide the shovel, and to never speak of it again."

"I got a slightly different version," Granny Bert said. "I got the that's-where-the-bodies-are-buried version."

"What on earth!" Virgie cried.

"I'm not ashamed to admit it. It gave me quite a shakeup."

"I can see why. She didn't say such a thing to me, but she did act mighty upset about the shovel. I wonder what she's talking about?"

"Who knows? It could be something that actually happened, or something she saw on a movie."

"She has an active imagination, that's for sure. Told me some mighty tall tales. Some may have been true, but I could tell she embellished some of the stories. The tales were harmless, mind you, unless she told them at Sunday morning services."

"Good thing Wanda is sitting with her today. We'll have to come up with some reason Sybil can't take Monday. Thank the good Lord tomorrow is Saturday, and the bank is closed."

"I'm planning to go to Bryan Monday and shop for a new dress. I guess I can ask her to come along and give me her opinion."

"That sounds like a good idea," Granny Bert agreed. "If anyone appreciates a pretty dress, it's Sybil."

"I do worry a bit about Wanda. Turning her

and Ella loose together may not be such a good idea. And we'd better warn her about the backyard. Knowing our friend, she just may take a shovel and dig the tree up on her own!"

"True. You call and warn her about going outside, and I'll check in on them later in the day."

"Sounds like a plan."

Even the best-laid plans often went astray.

Virgie couldn't reach Wanda when she called, and then she forgot to try again later.

When Granny Bert called after lunch to check on them, Wanda didn't pick up her phone. After three tries, Granny Bert got worried and decided to drive out there to see for herself if everything was okay.

No one had ever accused Wanda Shanks of being conventional. When she had walked in on her husband and another woman in bed, Wanda had quietly walked back into the living room, pulled the old shotgun down from above the mantel, returned to the bedroom, and proceeded to run that 'low-down, lying weasel and his two-bit hussy' out of her house and down the street, both of them butt naked. She loved dancing, margaritas, and 'medicinal' marijuana, especially when combined. Her short hair was dyed a harsh black, and she wore her clothes too tight, despite her generously sized figure. Nothing was too daring for her to do or say. In a community where people loved to gossip, Wanda was more than happy to give them something to talk about.

Granny Bert had long told herself that nothing Wanda could do would surprise her anymore, but that afternoon, her friend proved her wrong.

When no one answered her knock, Granny Bert let herself in through the unlocked door. "Wanda? Ella? Are you two in here?" Hearing no answer, she ventured into the kitchen.

Nothing seemed out of place. Two plates and glasses were turned upside-down in the drainboard, the pleasant smell of a recent meal still lingered in the air, and a broom and empty dustpan leaned against one wall. Everything looked good, until she spotted the tequila bottle on the table.

"Oh, Lord. What has Wanda done now?" Granny Bert groaned.

Hearing raucous laughter coming from the other room, she hurried through the door. She stopped short when she saw the sight in front of her.

Wanda and Ella were playing the game Twister, of all things, and they had somehow tangled themselves up into a knot.

"What are you two doing in here? Have you lost your mind, Wanda Shanks?" she demanded.

"No, but I lost feeling in my leg about ten minutes ago. Ella says she got a cramp, and it cut off her blood supply, so she's paralyzed from the waist down. Now neither one of us can move." They both laughed like the situation was hilarious.

"Exactly how much tequila did you two have?"

"How much was in the bottle?" Wanda hedged.

"It was almost empty."

"Oops. It was full when we started."

"What if Banisha comes home and finds you like this?" Granny Bert glared at her.

"Then she can help us get untangled, unless you want to do the honors."

"Lord have mercy, woman! We should have known better than to leave you here unsupervised! Neither one of you are in your right mind."

"She sure does like to gripe, don't she?" Ella asked her new best friend.

"She's mostly harmless," Wanda assured her. "Unless you get her riled. Then all bets are off."

"You'd better call off the bets, then, because I'm riled!" Granny Bert informed her. "Give me your hand."

"If I move either one, I'll fall and squash this poor woman to death," Wanda said. "Better save the scrawny one first."

It took crawling in under her friend on her belly, massaging Ella's back until her muscles unclenched, untangling one of her spindly legs from around one of Wanda's thick thighs, facing sights and smells no one should ever be forced to endure, and—Lord help her—unfastening Wanda's bra as one of the straps was mysteriously wound around both of their arms. After twelve minutes of grueling labor, Granny Bert finally pulled Ella out by her armpits. They collapsed on the rug just before Wanda came crashing down.

She was still laughing when she hit the floor, face-first.

Even Ella sat up before Granny Bert could catch her breath. "Whoo-wee! That was fun!" she proclaimed. "Can we play that again tomorrow?"

"Neither one of us may be able to move tomorrow," Wanda predicted.

"That's because I may kill you," Granny Bert threatened.

"I'll get the shovel," Ella offered.

Once they managed to get off the floor, Wanda mopped her face with the hem of her skirt. Along with the smells, that was one of the nightmarish sights Granny Bert had endured.

"Lord a mercy, I worked up a sweat."

"You'd better get this mess cleaned up and wipe that goofy smile off your face before Banisha gets home. And put your bra back on!"

"You're the one who took it off."

"Not by choice, I can assure you! I'm going to the kitchen to make a pot of coffee. With any luck, it will sober you two up. And," she jabbed a finger in Wanda's sweaty face, "you'd best pray Ella forgets to tell Banisha about this little game of yours, or we'll be out of a job."

"Oh, she'll forget," Wanda said with confidence. "She can't even remember where she put her shovel."

Granny Bert grumbled the entire time she was in the kitchen. By the time she had a tray loaded with the coffee pot and three cups, she had calmed down enough to keep her temper in check. But when she returned to the living room with her tray and found the room empty, her temper skyrocketed again.

Wanda had taken Ella out to the back porch.

"See that spot yonder?" Ella pointed with a smile. "That's where my pappy had his garden. Why, you never did see such a green thumb as that man's! He grew peas, tators, onions, squash, cabbage—"

"And pumpkins," Granny Bert broke in, trying hard to remain calm. "Don't forget the pumpkins. But I have our coffee ready, and it's in the living room. Let's go back in before it gets cold."

"It's not cold out here," Wanda objected. "It's a beautiful day."

"I meant the coffee. I know how you hate cold coffee."

"That's true. But Ella wanted to sit out here, so why don't we drink our coffee here on the porch?"

"I don't think that's a good idea. Let's go inside."

"I think it's a great idea. Stop being a party pooper and sit out here with us."

"Trust me, Wanda, that's not a good idea."

"But Ella's trying to remember where she put her shovel. I thought coming out here might jog her memory."

"Again, you don't want to do that," Granny Bert warned.

Ella spoke over them, her tone emphatic. "I didn't *put* my shovel nowhere. I hid it, just like my Pappy told me to do."

"Oh, Lord, look what you've done now," Granny Bert muttered. "Come on, Wanda, help me get her into the house before she gets cranked up."

"Cranked up? What are you talking about?

What's the harm in reliving a few old memories? Go on, Ella. Tell me all about your pappy and his garden."

Ella started over, telling about her father's many plants. She threw Granny Bert a sassy look as she included the pumpkins this time.

"And see that spot there? That's where the well stood. The purest, sweetest water on this earth. I can still taste it. Cool and wet, on a hot summer's day. Nothing better." She breathed in a serene sigh as she recalled the memory.

"See?" Wanda whispered. "Where's the harm in making her happy, thinking about the good old days?"

Ella's eyes popped back open. "See that big tree yonder?" she asked.

"The tall pin oak?"

"That's the one. It's evil," Ella said.

"Okay, let's go in now," Granny Bert broke in.

"Hush up!" Ella snarled. "I'm telling my friend here something important. That tree right there is pure evil. I'm telling you the truth, girl. Don't ever go near it. Do you understand?"

"I—I think so," Wanda said. Clearly, she didn't understand a thing, but she was willing to go along if it meant hearing a good story.

"Don't. Go. Near. It," Ella stressed. "It's evil. Pure evil."

"Tree. Evil. Stay away." Wanda nodded, her too-dark hair dancing with the gesture. "Got it."

"It gets worse," Granny Bert said out of the side of her mouth. "Let's go back in."

"We lost a good shovel that day," Ella went on, almost conversationally. "My pappy told me to hide it good, so I did."

"Why did you have to hide it?" Wanda asked.

"Because it had blood on it, you fool!"

"Bl—Blood?" Wanda no longer looked amused. She looked spooked, especially at the harsh way Ella addressed her.

"Yes, blood. It was everywhere. I burned our clothes, but all I could do was hide the shovel."

"Of—Of course," Wanda agreed weakly. "That makes sense."

"Nothing made sense about that day!" Ella shouted. "Nothing!"

"Okay, we're going inside now," Granny Bert said in a firm voice. "Wanda, help me get Ella in."

"I'm not going anywhere, except down there to dig up the body!" she insisted.

"Body? What body?" Wanda's eyes widened.

"As soon as I find my shovel, I'll show it to you."

"I—I don't want to dig up a body." Wanda sounded frantic. "I want coffee. Don't you want coffee, Ella? Bertha, I know you want some. Right?"

"I sure do. Come with us, Ella, and we'll all have a cup of nice, hot coffee."

"And cookies?" Ella asked hopefully, all traces of her surly self gone. "Because if we're having coffee, I like cookies with mine."

"Of course, of course. And if we don't have any, I'll whip up a batch real quick."

"Your cookies won't taste like Gracie's," the

woman predicted. "Gracie made the best cookies in the world."

"Tell us about Gracie's cookies, Ella," Wanda said.

They had managed to get her over the threshold, but at the mention of Gracie's name, she balked. "Don't you ever say her name, do you hear me? Never!"

Wanda cringed. "My bad."

"I've told you. I don't talk about her. I don't *ever* talk about her, and don't you, either!"

And so the afternoon went, until both Ella and Wanda passed out on the couch, leaving Granny Bert to collapse in the nearby chair, fully spent.

14

Brash's old friend Kent Bergman had hosted a fish fry from their catch on his boat, and the party had lasted late. Kent had a friendly wife and two teenagers of his own, so the entire family had a good time.

Brash and Madison were still asleep the next morning when Blake woke them with an insistent, "Mom! Daddy D! Wake up. I gotta talk to you."

Madison turned over groggily, mumbling something about the early morning hour. "Can't it wait?"

"No, it can't! I just got a text from Lindsey."

"Really, son? This can't wait?" his mother asked groggily.

"No! She's really upset."

Brash opened one eye. "Now it's Lindsey? Really, Blake?"

"Would you two just wake up? I need to talk to you!"

They unwillingly did as he asked, propping up against the bed's headboard and opening their sleep-filled eyes.

"We're awake now," Madison yawned. "What is it?"

"Patty's missing," Blake blurted out.

"Missing?" Brash came instantly awake. "What do you mean, missing?"

"She's not in the house. She's not answering her phone. They have no idea where she's gone. Lindsey is freaking out!"

"Okay, okay. Let's not panic," Brash said. "Why don't you go make us some coffee, and your mom and I will join you in a minute? Let us put some clothes on, at least."

A few minutes later, they came into the common room wearing leftover Christmas pajamas and tousled hairstyles. Blake motioned to their coffee, already waiting for them on the coffee table.

"Thank you," Madison said, sinking onto the couch with a cup. "Now, start from the top. They can't find Patty?"

"No! They have no idea where she is."

Before he could go on, the girls tumbled from their room, phones in hand.

"Ohmygosh!" Bethani said. "Patty's missing!"

"Lindsey just called us," Megan rushed to add. "She's hysterical!"

"Blake was just telling us. You girls sit down and tell us what you know," Brash said.

They all started talking at once, until their father put up his hand. "Hold on. Blake... you go first."

"Lindsey texted me just before I woke you up.

There's no sign of her."

"When was the last time anyone saw her?" Madison asked.

Megan waved her hand to be next. "Last night. She and Rachel stayed up late, having a heart to heart." She cut her eyes over to Blake. "Everything was good, and they said good night. They rented houses next door to one another, with a catwalk that connects the two decks. The last Rachel saw her, Patty was at the end of the catwalk, stepping onto her deck. They waved good night, and Rachel went inside."

"That was the last anyone saw of her," Bethani picked up the story. "Lindsey said her bed was still made—she actually makes her bed every morning—and it doesn't look like she even came in last night. Somewhere between the deck and the house, she just... vanished."

"And no one else in the house has seen her?" Brash questioned.

"Lindsey's dad and Lance are out looking for her. Josh and Brandon are driving along the beach, thinking she may have gone for a walk and fallen or... something." His voice trailed off, but they all knew the *something* wasn't good.

"I guess all the cars and golf carts are accounted for?" Brash asked.

"Yes. That was the first thing Mr. Lewis did."

"They keep calling her phone, but she won't pick up," Bethani said.

"The battery could be out by now," her mother said. "Maybe she's stranded somewhere and can't call for them to come get her."

"That's what they're hoping."

Brash had to ask. "Have they called the police?"

"Not yet." Megan shook her head. "Lindsey said Patty isn't one to just wander off, but she also isn't one to make a scene. Lindsey said the last thing she'd want is for someone to make a big deal over something that probably has a logical explanation."

"She's been gone overnight. That's a big deal," Madison disagreed.

"Yeah, but Lindsey's mom said the police probably won't see it that way. She's in college, down here on Spring Break, yada, yada. They'd say she probably met up with a guy, and there was no reason to overreact."

"Do they honestly think that's what happened?" Even to Madison, that sounded farfetched. She barely knew the girl, but she found it hard to believe Patty could be so irresponsible.

"No," Megan admitted. "But Mrs. Lewis used to be a police dispatcher. She says she knows how the system works. The police don't normally get involved unless it's been over twenty-four hours, or a threat has been made."

"She's not wrong," Brash sighed.

"Can't *you* do something, Daddy D?" Blake wanted to know.

"I could go over to their house," he agreed. "See if I can help in any way."

The relief on all three teens' faces was visible. "That would be great," Megan said.

"You're the best. I'll text Lindsey and tell her," Blake said.

"It will take me a few minutes to get dressed. And at least another cup of coffee."

"I'll make it," Bethani offered, jumping to her feet. "Can we go, too?"

"I think it would be best if you kids stayed here," he told them.

"But—"

He cut into her protest. "Think of this. What if Patty shows up here to talk? She might be too embarrassed to go back to the house, or she might think she's in trouble. She may need your support before she faces them."

"He's right," Megan said with a vigorous nod. "We should stay here, just in case."

Bethani reluctantly agreed as she made the coffee.

"I think I'll take the golf cart and look on this end of the beach," Blake said.

"And Beth and I will hang out on the deck to watch for her," said Megan.

Everyone left to get dressed, and the kids dispersed on their missions. Over another cup of fortification, Madison asked her husband, "You put on a calm show for the kids but tell me what you really think."

Brash frowned. "I think Patty didn't just wander off."

"Me, either."

There was a knock on their door, and Madison looked hopeful. "Maybe it's her!"

She hurried to open it, surprised to see Sirenity there. She had a worried expression on her face.

"We need to talk," she said without preamble. "Can we come in?"

"We?" Madison looked behind her, hoping to see the missing girl.

She certainly wasn't expecting the man who stepped over their threshold. Bob Smith followed Sirenity inside, wearing the familiar hat pulled low. He kept his face averted until he was inside, and the door closed behind them.

"May I introduce you to our other guest, Mr. Smith," Sirenity said. "And these are my friends I told you about, Brash and Madison deCordova. I think they can help you if you'll let them."

Madison held her facial expression in check when Bob Smith pulled off his hat and raised his head. His face was scarred, and one cheek was disfigured, pulling his nose slightly to one side. His neck was ravaged with more scars, the twisted skin trailing down to disappear beneath the neck of his pullover shirt. Even his hands bore marks of burns and cuts.

"Hello," he said in a voice as rough as his skin.

"Please, come on inside," Madison invited, motioning to the couches.

"Smith," Brash acknowledged, extending his hand in greeting. "Sirenity." He nodded her way.

"Can I offer you something to drink? Coffee? Water?" Madison asked.

"Water, please," Smith answered.

Sirenity turned down the offer. "I'm good."

Once Madison was back and settled on the couch beside him, Brash addressed the man across from them. "What can we do for you, Bob Smith?" he asked.

Smith looked nervous, until Sirenity prodded him with a soft, "You can trust them."

He took a gulp of water before letting out a deep breath and plunging ahead.

"As you can guess," he said, darting his eyes to Brash's, "my name isn't Bob Smith. My real name is Samuel Roberts, and I'm a chemical engineer. I used to work for Tar-Go Chemicals as one of their top chemists." He motioned to his face. "This was my severance pay for eleven years of loyalty and dedication."

Seeing the look of horror on Madison's face, he said brusquely, "I don't need your sympathy. I need your help."

"How?" Brash asked.

"Seventeen years ago, I discovered a flaw in the process Tar-Go used in one of their refineries. I warned them of the mistake and told them how to correct it. I urged them to take action, but they said it would cost too much money, and their old method worked fine. I reported them to the Texas Railroad Commission, but before I could present my evidence, there was a horrible explosion at the plant. A lot of lives were lost that day, but it could have been prevented if they had only listened to me." Clearly distraught, he ran his scarred hands over his head until he cradled it between his palms.

"I tried," he insisted. "God knows I tried, but they wouldn't listen. And then the explosion happened, and it was so horrible. People were running and screaming. I tried to save the ones I could. I found one man trapped under a huge section of pipe, but the flames were so high... I couldn't save him." A sob escaped him. "I burned my face, trying to get him free, but in the end, I had to leave him. I'm still tortured by his screams." He rocked back and forth, trying to block the image from his mind.

"I got out," he finally said, composing himself. "But there were others who weren't so lucky. And some of us who did survive, like me, almost wished we hadn't. The recovery process was grueling. Surgery after surgery. Months of rehabilitation and physical therapy." He stopped talking and waved his hand in front of him, as if brushing the details away.

"But that's not what I need to tell you. I need to tell you what happened after. After the explosion, and after the cover-ups, and after the denials by Tar-Go, they refused to take the blame for what happened. And they whisked me away to some hospital in Mexico, where I had excellent care, all bills paid, but where they just left me." He took another gulp of water to soothe his permanently parched throat. "Between the trauma and the pain and all the different medicine I was on, my memory was gone. I had no identification on me, so they called me Juan Perez. It was eleven months before I remembered my own name, and what had happened. Even then, some of the details were fuzzy."

"That's awful!" Madison couldn't hold the sentiment in any longer. "They just abandoned you in a strange country?"

"They couldn't risk me remembering and coming back to the States. With no passport and no proof of my American citizenship, I wasn't allowed to cross the border. Not legally."

"It may be best I don't know the details," Brash said. "But, obviously, you made it home."

"Yes, but I couldn't exactly *go* home. My wife most likely thought I was dead. And how could I show up on her doorstep, looking like this? Believe me, it took years for the scars to even look this good."

'Good' was never a word Madison would use to describe his appearance, but she wisely kept her mouth shut. Her heart went out to the man and all he had been through.

"Besides, she had moved away, and I had no idea where she went. I started going by the name Bob Smith, and I kept on the move, hoping Tar-Go would never find me. And, eventually, as my full memory returned, I contacted a lawyer."

Seeing his glass was empty, Sirenity took the liberty of refilling it so that Madison and Brash could focus on his story.

"Long story short," Samuel Roberts continued, "we went to the officials, and eventually, to the DA. They wanted me to testify in court against Tar-Go, but I refused until they could locate my family and assure me they were safe. Loretta was living in Lufkin by then, raising our child alone.

"There was a ton of litigation against the

company—wrongful death suits, personal injury, permanent disability, that sort of thing—but they had the best lawyers in the country working for them. They kept the case tied up in the system for years. And they never knew I was back, living under the name Bob Smith, until the DA finally got the charges to stick. They sent me to live in a series of safe houses but somehow, Tar-Go found me, and they threatened to hurt my family if I testified against them."

"So, you slipped away to see for yourself that your family was safe," Brash surmised.

"Exactly. I knew my daughter went to Sam Houston—once they located Loretta, I had kept up with them through the years—and I knew she was coming here for Spring Break, so I followed." He ran his hand over his head again. "I don't know what I planned to do. I wanted to talk to her, but I wasn't sure how she would receive me. I hadn't been in her life for years. She probably thought I was dead. Or worse, a deadbeat dad. I just wanted her to know I loved her and why I had stayed away all those years. I mean, if Tar-Go found me, they couldn't afford to let me live. I knew this might be my only chance to ever speak to my daughter. But then you," he looked at Brash, "told me someone had followed me here, and I couldn't risk it. I decided I had to go back, if only to pull them away from her."

"Yet you're still here."

He nodded. "I was packing my suitcase when someone delivered this to my door." He handed Brash a manila envelope.

There was a grainy photograph inside, obviously taken at night. The details were hard to distinguish, but that was definitely Patty in the picture. Her hands and feet were bound, and there was a gag around her mouth. A simple note warned 'Do not involve the police, or she pays the price. You know what to do.'

"They have my daughter!" Roberts sobbed.

Brash nodded gravely. "We heard about Patty."

"You—You knew she was my daughter?"

"We suspected as much." Brash shifted his attention to Sirenity. "Did you see who delivered this note?"

"No," she said, almost as distraught as her guest. "No, I didn't. The doors are locked from ten at night until six in the morning. Guests can get in with their keycards during that time, but anyone can come in after that. I have deliveries, surprise inspections, walk-ins hoping to book a room, all sorts of things. I must have been in the kitchen when they came in. I never heard them go up the stairs."

"It's okay. You don't have to defend yourself," Madison assured her friend.

"Any chance of getting prints off this are already shot," Brash said, handing the photograph to Sirenity. "Do you recognize where this might have been taken?"

She studied the picture. "It's hard to say. It was taken in the dark, and the quality isn't good."

"Obviously, they nabbed her at night, after she and Rachel parted. Her kidnapper must have been waiting for her on the deck, hidden in the shadows," Madison guessed.

"Have you talked to her friends?" Sirenity asked. "Do they know she was kidnapped?"

Brash answered. "To my knowledge, at the moment, they're just saying she's missing. They're out looking for her now. In fact," he said, "I was about to head over there, myself, and offer my assistance."

"You can't go to the police!" the frantic father insisted.

"I don't know if Sirenity told you this or not," Brash said, his voice softening, "but I *am* the police. I have no jurisdiction here, but I do have experience in the matter. And it is imperative that you tell me anything, *anything*," he stressed, "that might help us find her."

"Us?" His voice pitched higher in with panic. "You can't go to the police! You saw the note. You know what they'll do if I involve the police!"

"Smith. Roberts," he corrected, "you know it's the right thing to do."

"And look what doing the right thing has gotten me so far!" He got up to pace the floor. "No, you cannot go to the local police. If you do, I'll—I'll—okay, I don't know what I'll do, but it won't be good, and it will be on you, Brash deCordova." He stabbed his finger in the air, aimed at Brash.

"Okay," Brash ground out. "For now, we'll try to handle this on our own. But you have to tell me. Is there *anything* you haven't told us?"

"No. No! Nothing. I swear, that's all I know. I don't even know who's following me. You're the one who saw him, not me. I had no idea I was being tailed."

Brash believed him, so he turned back to Sirenity. "If you needed to hide someone on the peninsula, can you think of somewhere you might go?"

"I can think of a hundred places," she said rather hopelessly. "There are swamps and bayous all around here, especially over on Goat Island. You can only get there by boat, but people have fishing camps over there. Any of those places would be secluded. Then there's Anahuac Wildlife Refuge, not to mention Fort Travis. The gates are locked at dark on both places, but of course, there's always a way in, especially by water. The old batteries at the fort are kept gated and locked, but they would make an excellent place to hide. There's also a lot of desolate, uninhabited areas along the peninsula, especially down on the west end. And of course, the bird sanctuary comes to mind, which backs up to the washout. The beach area of the washout is party central. It can get rowdy down there at times, but when it's empty, it's empty. No houses, no lights, just the marsh and the bayous on one side, and the ocean on the other." She sent Samuel Roberts an apologetic look. "Some bad stuff has happened down there."

He gave a curt nod. "Bad stuff happens everywhere."

15

Brash and Madison both met with the Lewis family. Their friends, the Glenwoods, had come over, as well, so the house was full. The kids were out on the deck, willing their phones to ring, while Brash did his best to keep everyone calm.

"I told them it probably won't do any good to call the police yet," Tina Lewis said. "It's Spring Break, and kids will be kids, they'll say. It's not fair, but we both know that's how it is."

"Unfortunately, I think you're right," Brash agreed. "Have you called Patty's mom?"

"Not yet," Tina admitted. "I'm hoping she'll still show up, and her mom will be worried for nothing. I've only met her once, during freshmen orientation when our girls were assigned as roommates, but she seemed a little... high strung. That's a long way for her to drive when she's hysterical."

"We could probably arrange for an escort," Brash thought aloud. "I have a buddy who's on the sheriff's department in Angelina County."

"But then they would coordinate with the Galveston County Sheriff, and I thought we weren't calling them in yet," Madison pointed out.

"True."

"Mom! Dad! I just got a message!" Lindsey yelled, racing into the house. She was in such a rush, she almost ran into the door. Her breath came in gulps. "Patty isn't just missing. She's been kidnapped!" the young woman wailed.

"Kidnapped?" Brenda Glenwood gasped.

"What kind of message?" Neal Lewis asked his daughter. "Let me see it. Let Mr. deCordova see it!" He motioned for Brash to go first.

"It came from Patty's phone," Lindsey explained. Her hands shook so hard, she almost dropped the phone as she transferred the device to Brash.

It was the same photo sent to Samuel Roberts. The digital quality was somewhat better than the printed copy had been, but it still lacked much to be desired. He could make out the grassy area behind her and what looked like a poorly constructed shelter, for lack of a better word. It was more like a couple of boards with a sheet of warped plywood. At least, that was his best guess. Again, the lighting and the quality were terrible.

There was a piece of paper propped up against her.

'No cops,' it said, in the same block lettering as the one sent to her father.

Brash airdropped the photo to himself and to Madison and handed the device over to Neal Lewis.

"What should we do?" the man asked frantically.

"For now, let's do as they say. No police. If they make contact again, let me know immediately, even if it's in the middle of the night," Brash instructed.

"She has to stay out there another night?" Lindsey shrieked. "She must be terrified!"

"Let's hope I figure out where she is before that. Lindsey, can we talk for a minute? I need to ask you some questions."

"In here?" she asked nervously.

"Of course, unless there's a reason you'd like to speak to me in private." There was a question in his eyes.

"No, of course not. I—I'd rather my parents be here."

"As would I. Here, let's sit down and try to relax."

"Relax? My roommate is out there somewhere! She's been—She's been kidnapped! How can I relax?" Lindsey dissolved into tears.

Her mother rushed to her side, pulling her into her arms. "Do we really have to do this right now?" she asked Brash.

"You know how important the first twenty-four hours are. Yes, we need to do this."

"Very well," she sighed. She settled more comfortably beside her daughter. "Okay, honey," she told the dark-haired beauty, "you need to answer his questions as honestly and openly as you can. No one will judge you, or Patty. Just tell him everything you know."

"But I don't know anything!" Lindsey insisted.

Brash sat beside her, just far enough away to give her some space. "When you were at college, did Patty seem upset about anything recently? Nervous, maybe?"

"A little," Lindsey sniffed, holding a tissue to her face. "She's always been a worrywart, but right after the new semester, she started getting... I don't know... antsy. She's never been much of a social butterfly but after that, getting her out of the dorm took an act of Congress. She always said she had to study, but she spent most of her time looking out the window. I asked her if she was seeing someone, but she said no. I even asked if someone was harassing her, but she denied that, too. But I'm not sure I believed that."

"Why do you say that?" Brash asked in a conversational manner, versus his usual interrogative style.

"She just seemed... different. I asked if something happened over Christmas break, but she said no. Honestly? At first, I thought she was homesick. That happened to another girl on our hall. She ended up dropping out of college and going back home. I didn't want that happening to Patty. She's so smart and so sweet." A fresh bout of tears fell. "She doesn't deserve this! Not Patty!"

Rachel stood behind her friend, touching her shoulder and crying along with her.

"And she never said what was bothering her?" Brash asked.

"No. But she was really excited about coming

down here this week, and she seemed so relaxed the first day or so. But then the night we had the weenie roast… she kept staring off into the shadows. At one point, she asked if anyone else smelled cigarette smoke. We all just laughed. We were having a weenie roast, and smoke is smoke, right? But maybe we shouldn't have laughed at her. Maybe she knew something we didn't. And now I feel awful because what if that was a clue or something?"

"Rachel?" Brash asked, shifting his gaze to the other young woman. "Last night, when you and Patty were on the deck, do you remember smelling cigarette smoke?"

"I don't—I don't think so," she said with a fair share of uncertainty. "But, I do remember at one point, Patty sort of sniffed the air. I didn't think anything of it. Do you—Do you think it was something? Did I miss something important?" she worried.

"No, of course not. Would you mind telling me about your conversation? You don't have to share anything too personal, but it's important I get a feel for her mood and the frame of mind she may have been in. Did she seem distracted to you? Worried?"

"Only about—" Rachel flickered a glance at Madison. "—Blake. I don't suppose he told you anything about that?"

"A little," Brash acknowledged.

"Your son is very cute," she admitted. "And very nice. And I thought we had a nice rapport going. But then we hung out at the inn, and he sat by Patty all night. I admit, I—I was a little jealous. I adore

Patty. I go to Blinn College, but I've visited Lindsey and Patty a ton of times at their dorm. She's quiet but really funny when you get to know her. And I didn't want to mess our friendship up, even over a great guy like Blake. Which he pointed out, after I sort of picked a fight with Patty."

She looked sick about their argument, realizing now how petty it had been. "But we had a long heart to heart last night, and we both agreed that we would all just be friends. We may never see Blake again, but Patty and I will still see each other, and we don't want things to be weird between us. So, yeah, things were great when we parted. We hugged and said goodnight, and she waved to me as she went over the walkway. And that—that's the last time I saw her!" Rachel sobbed. She clung to her mother, who had come to stand beside her. Her father clumsily patted her back, looking completely helpless.

"What do we do, Mr. deCordova?" Neal Lewis asked, his own voice rough with emotion. "Tell us how we can help."

"I have a couple of ideas," Brash said. "I need to go check them out, but please, if you hear anything, contact me immediately."

"Of course, of course. And thank you. Thank you for coming."

Madison hugged the girls and their mothers as Brash shook hands with the men, including the younger ones. Everyone was very appreciative for their help and concern, repeatedly telling them so.

Once they were away from the house,

Madison asked, "Do you really have any ideas, or was that just for their benefit?"

"A little of both. But mostly," he admitted, "it was to make all of us feel better."

"I sent the photo to Sirenity like you asked. She agreed it had a better quality, but she wanted to show it to a friend of hers. She said he was BOI, whatever that means."

"Born on island," Brash explained, "even though this is, technically, a peninsula."

Madison sighed. "Technicalities aside, I just hope he can help."

The moment they stepped into the suite, their own teens confronted them.

"Really, Mom? How could you!" Bethani demanded.

"Why didn't you tell us Patty had been *kidnapped*?" Megan cried, daring to poke her father in the chest. "We had to hear it from Lindsey and Rachel."

"Yeah," Blake sulked. "Low blow, Daddy D, Mom. Thanks for the show of confidence."

"It's not like that," Madison defended. "There's circumstances you don't know about."

"Yeah, like our friend has been kidnapped, while you let us go on looking for her, and waiting for her to call!" Bethani stormed.

"Sit down and just hear us out," Brash said. "What we're about to tell you can't leave this room. Patty's friends don't know this. I doubt even Patty herself knows this."

"Now you're just being dramatic," Megan accused, flopping onto one of the couches. Bethani and Blake fell into place beside her, both looking as glum and skeptical as she did.

In lieu of the other sofa, Madison sat in the chair, and Brash took the ottoman.

"You know about the two men who have been following your friends," their mother started.

"Yeah, Creepy and Creepier," Megan muttered.

"They're the ones who did this?" Blake asked in surprise.

"We think one of them is," Brash said.

"Wow. I just got a chill," Bethani whispered. "They were following *us*, too."

"Only because you were with Patty," her mother was quick to assure her.

"So, this has been about Patty all along?" Blake sounded confused. "But why? Like I said, she has to be the nicest girl on earth."

"It's not exactly about her. It's about her father."

"I knew it! I knew that guy in the long coat was a spy!" Blake jumped to his feet triumphantly. "Or with the mafia. He's the one, isn't he? He's the one who kidnapped Patty!"

"Not exactly," Brash said. "Sit back down. This may get complicated."

"The truth is," Madison explained, "the man we saw at the store, the one in the long coat and hat—"

"The guy staying here, right?" Megan clarified.

"Right. The one who said his name was Bob Smith."

"Bob Smith?" Blake scoffed. "Yeah, right. He should have just said John Q. Public."

"Or he could have used his real name, which is Samuel Roberts," Madison went on.

"Roberts? Isn't that Patty's name?"

"Yes. That's because Samuel Roberts is her father."

"The coat and hat guy?"

"That's the one."

"But we doubt Patty knows that," Brash put in. "She hasn't seen him since she was two years old. There's a good chance she doesn't even remember him."

"So, he just kidnapped his own daughter?" Bethani asked incredulously. "Why did he wait until she was almost grown? Wouldn't it have been easier to nab her as a child?"

"It's more complicated that than," Brash said. "Seventeen years ago, there was an explosion at a nearby oil refinery. Patty's father worked there as a chemical engineer. He knew there was something wrong with one of the plant's procedures, and he warned his bosses it could end badly, but they didn't listen. They pushed ahead because the old way was more cost effective."

Blake stated the obvious, "Not if there was an explosion!"

"I think I read something about that downstairs," Bethani murmured.

"It was a horrible ordeal, and a lot of people lost their lives that day. A lot more were injured, some of them for life. Patty's father was one of them. If you saw him up close, you'd know he was left with some severe scars and burns all over his body."

"That's why he wears all the weird clothes?" Bethani asked. "Now I feel bad for making fun of him."

"That's part of the reason," her mother agreed. "The other part is because he's been incognito for the past seventeen years."

Blake looked excited. "He really is a spy?"

"No. He's hiding from the spy."

"You lost me."

"The other guy, the one smoking the cigarette, has been following Mr. Smith—I mean, Mr. Roberts," Madison corrected. "He works for Tar-Go Chemicals, the one who owned the refinery."

"So, *he's* the spy." Blake tried to follow along.

"I guess you could call him that. He was hired to keep Roberts from testifying when the case finally goes to court next month."

"There *is* a hit man!" he exclaimed with a fist pump. "I just pegged the wrong guy."

Brash frowned at Blake's misplaced enthusiasm. "That's one way to describe him, I suppose. But, son, this is no laughing matter. That man was sent here to stop Roberts, using whatever method was necessary. Even if that meant kidnapping an innocent young woman who knows nothing about this."

"Oh, yeah," he said, crestfallen. "I didn't think

about that. Poor Patty. She didn't do anything to deserve this."

"Neither did her father," Madison reminded him. "He tried to do the right thing. He spotted the problem, came up with a way to fix it, and reported it to the right people, only to be ignored. He even went to the authorities but by then, it was too late. In the aftermath of the explosion, while he was recovering in a hospital in Mexico, Tar-Go swept the whole thing under the rug. It was years before he found someone to help him."

"What took him so long?" Megan asked. "And why Mexico?"

"Long story," Madison said. "The bottom line is, he's ready to testify, but they can't let that happen. Not if the company wants to stay in business. And they think the best way to get to him is through his daughter."

"Oh, wow," Bethani breathed. "This is really bad."

"It is," Brash agreed. "That's why we didn't tell you at first. It wasn't our secret to tell. Roberts came to us this morning, after you three were gone. At the time, not even the Lewises knew she had been kidnapped. We thought it was best to keep a lid on it for as long as possible."

"I'm sorry." Megan's tone was sheepish. "We shouldn't have jumped to conclusions. We should have trusted you."

"She's right. We should have," Bethani echoed.

Blake agreed with his sisters. "You were doing what you thought was best."

"And we still are," Brash said. "We're going to do everything we can to find Patty, but we can't involve the local police at this time. Her father made me promise, and I don't take promises lightly. We need you to keep this to yourself, but we also need you to encourage her friends and their parents to trust us. Stress that they can't go to the police, or they may put her life in danger. Her father's as well, but you can't tell them that. That stays between us, okay?"

"Sure. We'll do our part," Blake assured him.

"I know you'll find a way to save her, Daddy D," his twin agreed.

Her faith in him was humbling.

Brash just hoped he didn't let her down.

"Vina came through for us," Madison announced. While they waited on news from Sirenity's friend, she had checked her email.

"I never once doubted it."

"By now, we already know Smith really is Samuel Roberts. His story checks out. Everything he told us is true. And the man following him is probably Donovan Rivera, a known associate of Lawrence Taft."

"And Taft is...?" Brash asked expectantly.

"Right-hand man to Tar-Go's CEO and grandson of its founder, M.E. Tarkington, III. Naturally, neither of them can get their own hands dirty, so Tarkington tells Taft to take care of it. In turn, Taft has a couple of high-priced thugs on the payroll to take care of things that are beneath them."

"Naturally."

"One of his go-to guys is in Qatar right now, so that leaves Rivera as the most likely one to tail Samuel Roberts. Believe it or not, he's the lesser of the two evils. Kidnapping is rather mild compared to his associate's favored methods."

"I won't ask for clarification on that," Brash said.

"Thank you. Because I may not sleep tonight after reading this file. This is some heavy stuff."

"Anything else useful Vina could tell us?"

Madison perused the email again. "I don't think so. She included some pictures of Rivera, which I just sent to your phone and is the ping you hear now. Other than that, there isn't much. A few of his haunts, none of them here. There is one place he might take Roberts if he doesn't just kill him on the spot, but it's not the place in Patty's picture. I'm pretty sure that was taken here on the island—peninsula, whatever—but this place is a house. Sort of a safe house they keep in Houston, although I use the term 'safe' very loosely."

"You know," Brash said, getting up to wander about the room, "that's one thing that's been bothering me about all this. Why didn't Rivera just kill Roberts when he first tracked him down? Why let things go this far?"

"Hmm. Good question."

"There has to be a good answer, too. Some reason Rivera didn't just pop him and get it over with."

"That's a rather crude way of putting it,"

Madison disapproved.

"Murder is a rather crude business," he countered.

"You've got me there. Why do you think that is? Why didn't Rivera just kill him on sight?"

"I don't know. There's something he hasn't told us. And it may just be the key to this whole case."

Less than an hour later, Sirenity knocked on their door.

"Hey, come on in," Madison welcomed her friend. "We're just brainstorming, trying to come up with ideas on how to find Patty."

"I just talked with my friend. He had good news/bad news."

"Good news first."

"The good news is Kronk thinks he knows where the photo was taken."

"Kronk? Interesting name."

"Interesting man," Sirenity countered. "He claims he's a direct descendant of the Karankawa Indians, a native tribe that once inhabited the coast. He's lived here his entire life and knows the area like the back of his hand."

"The bad news?" Brash asked.

"He says it's the no man's land between the bird sanctuary and the washout. The one place I was hoping it wasn't."

"What's the makeshift structure?"

She made a face. "Drug shack. Shag shack. Worst of the worst shack."

"Shag shack." Brash was amused by the term. "What are we, in England?"

"It's a nicer way of saying what the local teens call it."

"Let's go with shag shack," Madison quickly decided. "How do we get there?"

"Very carefully. There's a lot of things to consider."

"Like?"

"Like snakes. The stray alligator or two. Drug dealers. Thugs. Rapists. If you're really lucky, just a couple of high beach bums."

"But if Patty's out there in the middle of all that, we have to rescue her!"

"Absolutely," Brash said, "but Sirenity's right. We can't just barge in there. We have to be smart about this. Because our number one threat is Rivera. He's not going to let us get anywhere near her. Not without Roberts in tow."

"Who's Rivera?"

"The second man," Madison answered, "the one smoking the cigarette."

"Will your friend take us there?" Brash asked.

"He said he would."

"When?"

"There's a concert at the washout tonight. There will be enough people there to keep your approach from being so obvious. It may also give this Rivera a false sense of safety. He probably won't expect you until well after midnight, when the party dies down."

Brash nodded, the wheels busy turning in his mind. "I think I have an idea. I need to go out for a little while."

"Where are you going?" Madison asked.

"I'll explain later. I need to talk to Roberts before I go. Then I want you two to keep an eye on him. Make sure he stays here at the inn."

"How, exactly, are we supposed to do that?" his wife cried incredulously.

"Don't worry. I've got this," Sirenity assured her with a wink.

16

Brash knocked on Roberts' door. The younger couple staying at the inn, the ones in the room at the end of the hall, had just stepped from their door. He waited until they had passed and gone down the stairs before he knocked again.

After the third knock, just as he was getting suspicious that Roberts wasn't inside, he heard movement from within.

"It's me, deCordova. Let me in."

With a grunt, Roberts opened the door and hurried him inside.

"Have you heard anything else?" Brash asked.

"No. You?"

"No. They sent the same picture to Patty's friends, with a warning not to call the cops. For now, they've agreed to go along."

"For now? And later?" Roberts worried.

"Let's hope there's not a later. I have an idea, and I'll need your help. But first, you have to level with me. What haven't you told me?"

"Nothing! I told you everything."

"I don't think so. There's something that doesn't add up, and I think it's whatever you've left out of the equation."

"I told you what I know."

"Except the reason why Rivera hasn't already put a bullet through you and be done with it."

"That's who's after me? Rivera?"

"I'm not positive, but I think so. You know him?"

"I know of him. He's bad news."

"Not as bad as his associate from what I hear, so consider yourself lucky."

Roberts ran his hand over his head. Seeing that his guard was down, Brash walked him back against the wall, getting in his face. "But luck won't save your daughter, Roberts," he said harshly. "The truth may. Tell me what you left out."

"N—"

"Don't say nothing!" Brash barked. He twisted a handful Roberts' shirt in his hand, making the neckline taut. "Tell me. If you want my help, be straight with me."

"You're—You're choking me."

"Hardly!" Brash said, but he released him all the same.

Roberts rubbed at his throat, the skin there more sensitive than most. "I—I have proof," he finally admitted. "That's what they're after."

"What kind of proof? And why didn't you tell me that to begin with?"

"I wasn't sure I could trust you. Tar-Go has spies everywhere."

Brash let that comment go. He would have done the same thing if one of his kids had been kidnapped. "What kind of proof do you have?"

"A flash drive. Plus, a hard drive with the files on it."

"How long have you had them?"

"Honestly? I forgot about them at first." He motioned for Brash to follow him further into the room. It was a much smaller version of their spacious suite, but it had a small sofa and a desk with a chair. Roberts took the chair.

"Like I told you, it took awhile for my memory to come back. And when I did remember, I had to be careful about retrieving my proof. I had it hidden in two separate locations, so that if they found one, I still had a backup."

"Smart on your part."

"I gave the DA an encrypted version. I'm the only one who knows the code. I refused to give them access until I knew my daughter was safe."

"But obviously, Tar-Go knows you still have the files."

"But they don't know where. And that's the only reason I'm still alive today and the only thing I have to bargain with in exchange for Patty's life."

"You may not need it," Brash told him. "I have an idea on how to get her back."

"What is it?"

"I'm like you. I'm not sure I can trust you. You may try to do something stupid, like try to stop me. Or worse, to tag along."

"But she's my daughter! I have a right to be

there!"

"And get all of us killed. No, Roberts. I went along with not calling the local police. You'll have to go along with doing this my way."

He didn't like it, but he grudgingly agreed. "Is there anything I can do to help?"

"Two things. One, I need your clothes. Keep what you're wearing, but give me everything else, including your coat and both hats. And two, promise you'll stay in your room."

Temperatures were falling as evening approached, and Patty was already shivering. She was cold and wet and afraid. She was trying to stay strong, but it was getting harder and harder to remain brave.

She and Rachel had had a good talk last night, and she was happy to know their friendship was still intact. She had felt a lightness she hadn't felt since her first day at the beach, until she caught a whiff of the smoke. It was that same sweet smell of tobacco she recognized from campus.

She knew he was out there, watching, but she thought she was safe. She was on the deck, with her friends and both houses just feet away. When she and Rachel parted, she hurried along the catwalk, stopping only to toss a wave over her shoulder. The door was right there.

She heard a noise and felt a sharp prick on her neck. That was it.

The next thing she knew, dawn was streaking

across the sky, and she was somewhere cold and damp. She could hear activity in the near distance, but when she tried calling for help, she discovered her mouth was bound and gagged. There were ropes on her hands and feet, tying her down to some sort of pallet beneath her, making it impossible for her to move.

She had endured the entire day like this, knowing people were so close and yet so far away. A man had come at some point, and he had taken the gag off her mouth, but he held a knife at her throat and told her not to scream. He offered her bottled water and something to eat, which she greedily accepted. He held them both for her, keeping her hands tied.

When she told him she had lost feeling in her limbs, he untied her hands, allowed her to move them about, and then retied them in a different position. He did the same with her feet. He kept the knife at her throat in case she tried to run or anything else stupid, like trying to kick him. Then he changed her position, tied the ropes back on her feet and across her mouth, and left her alone again.

And now the sun was descending, and she couldn't keep the tears at bay. She heard music, and laughter, but no one could hear her scream; no one could see her fighting against her restraints.

She was all alone.

17

THE SISTERS

"I'm calling an emergency meeting," Granny Bert told Derron.

"When?"

"As soon as we can all get there."

"Where? Here?" he squeaked. "Tonight?"

"You heard me. Did you not catch the emergency part?"

"GB," he protested, using his abbreviated name for her. "It's Friday night! I had plans."

"Wanda told me all about your plans," the old woman scoffed. "The two of you were doing mani-pedis with Arlene Kopetsky."

"I really do need a more discreet roomie," Derron muttered.

"Wanda Shanks doesn't have a discreet bone in her body," Granny Bert puffed. "Her whole life screams 'read me! I'm an open book!' You should have thought about that before you rented a room from her."

"True," he contemplated. "But if I moved, I sure would miss breakfast every morning and the foot rubs at night. The perks make up for the many shortcomings she has."

"She rubs your feet at night?"

"Of course. It helps me sleep better."

Granny Bert snorted. "That's the craziest thing I've ever heard!"

"Wait. Are you telling me you've never had one of her foot rubs? Let me tell you, GB, they are divine. That's the best part of mani-pedi night. You should come next time."

"When pigs fly and the cows jump over the moon," she proclaimed. "And not one minute before!"

"Well," Derron sniffed, "your loss."

"I'm calling the girls." Granny Bert was impatient to get the conversation back on track. "You can order the pizza. When you go to pick it up, remember to get a receipt. Madison can pay you back later. Oh, and order a medium pepperoni for Hank. Virgie won't have time to cook his supper."

"What am I, the errand boy?"

"I'm delegating. I'm the one who called the meeting, remember? I can't do everything by myself!"

"Who left you in charge?" he whined.

"I'm always in charge."

He couldn't argue with her logic, so he sighed and asked, "Our usual order?"

"Yes. Sybil made a batch of brownies today, so she's bringing dessert."

"Yum. See you in twenty."

"Better make it thirty. Wanda said she was going straight home and taking off her 'bindings.' You know it will take her a good ten minutes to get that bra back on."

Derron whistled a tune. "I'm not listening. Too much information for my delicate little ears."

"Just order the pizza," Granny Bert told him and hung up the phone.

Thirty minutes later, the emergency meeting convened.

"We have a problem," Granny Bert said.

"We sure do! They forgot to include the red pepper packets for my pizza," Wanda complained.

"You don't need them anyway," Derron told his roommate. "You know it gives you heartburn."

"Can we forget the red pepper and get back to business?" Virgie asked. "Hank's pizza is getting cold."

Granny Bert cut right to the chase. "As it turns out," she admitted to the group, "Ella Getty is more of a handful than we anticipated. I can see why she keeps getting kicked out of the old folks' homes."

"She's a cantankerous old biddy, that's for sure," Virgie agreed.

"Oh, I don't know about that," Wanda contradicted. Strings of cheese dripped from her pizza as she finished off another piece. "We were getting along like bandits before Bertha arrived."

"I don't know if that's because the two of you

are on the same wavelength mentally," her friend replied, "or because you got her snockered."

Sybil gasped. "Wanda! You got that poor woman drunk?"

"Not on purpose," Wanda defended herself. "I was teaching her how to play beer pong, except we were using tequila. It just sort of happened. She's a quick study!" Wanda beamed as she reached for another slice of pizza.

"Lord a' mercy," Sybil tsked.

"Other than a slight mishap while playing Twister, we were having a grand ol' time. Until we went out on the back porch. Things went downhill from there."

Virgie slapped a hand to her forehead. "Oh, my word! I forgot to warn you about the back porch! You didn't answer the first time I called, and I plumb forgot after that."

"And you talk about my memory," Wanda huffed. "It would have been nice if you had given me a head's up before the bride of Frankenstein came out."

Derron's head swiveled between the women. "What are y'all talking about? What did I miss?"

"Something about that backyard sets her off," Granny Bert told him. "I don't know what it is, but once she looks at that old pin oak, she turns into a different person."

"What's a tree have to do with anything?"

"She claims it's evil," Virgie said. "Starts talking all crazy."

"And it puts her in a terrible mood for the rest

of the day," Granny Bert added. "That's when she gets really hard to handle."

Derron shrugged. "So, don't take her back outside. Easy fix."

"Thank you for that, o wise one," Granny Bert cracked. She turned back to her friends. "The question is, what is it about that tree that sets her off?"

"It has something to do with her pappy," Wanda noted.

"I thought she never talked about him," Sybil said. "That Gracie person, either."

"*We* can't talk about him," Virgie corrected. "*She* keeps bringing them up. But like she did the other day with you, if we ask any questions, she jumps down our throat and closes up tighter than Wanda's girdle."

"I wish she had been wearing that girdle today," Granny Bert muttered. "I had to crawl in under her and rescue Ella."

"We won't ask," Virgie said, trying not to visualize it in her head.

"Good. Like Ella, I don't want to talk about it."

"Who is this Gracie person?" Sybil wondered.

"That's what I'd like to know. I sure would like her recipe for cookies and cracklin cornbread," Wanda said. "Ella claims she made the best she ever tasted."

"When Banisha came home from work, I tried to find out more about her mother," Granny Bert told the group. "She didn't volunteer much, but she did say Ella's maiden name was Marsh. Does that ring a bell with any of you?"

"Ella Marsh." Sybil tried the name out. "Ella Marsh. No, I can't say it does."

"I don't think I've ever heard that name," Wanda agreed.

"Me, either," Virgie agreed. "But either she lived here at one point in her life, or that backyard reminds her of some place she did live."

"I think she lived here," Granny Bert said. "She's too familiar with the old house and with the layout of that backyard. She can point to exactly where all the crops were planted and where the well was."

"And where the bodies were buried," Virgie mumbled.

"Bodies?" Derron screeched. "What bodies?"

"That's what I'd like to know," Granny Bert said.

Virgie nodded. "She kept asking me where I hid the shovel. Her voice sounded like she was possessed by the devil. Kept calling me 'girl.'"

"I've always wanted to do an exorcism!" Wanda said, bouncing excitedly in her seat. "Can we? Can we do one on her?"

Granny Bert sighed. "No, Wanda, we can't. And I don't think she's possessed. I think she's reliving something bad that happened in her life. Something that took place right there at that house."

"Then count me out!" Derron proclaimed, throwing up his hands. "I don't do creepy."

"I'm not sure I want to go back, either," Sybil admitted, her dark eyes wide.

Her best friend nodded. "Virgie and I already talked about that. And I think the three of us can handle the schedule without you." She threw a scathing look at Wanda. "Well, maybe just the two of us. I'm not sure it's a good idea to send that one back."

"But Ella *likes* me!" Wanda protested. "She called you a fuddy-duddy."

"We're there to take care of her, not help her break a hip playing Twister."

"I didn't know you played," Derron perked up as he eyed his roommate. "Can we play that tomorrow night?"

"I already promised Arlene we'd reschedule our mani-pedis for tomorrow night. I don't want to smudge my polish."

"Could we quit talking about y'all's pathetic social life and get back to business? Unlike the rest of you, I have a husband to get back to!" Virgie huffed.

"I agree," Granny Bert said. "Sybil, since you won't be sitting with Ella, you can do most of the snooping for us. Find out if anyone remembers a Marsh family and what exactly happened out at the farm."

"Do you happen to know what her father's name was? What about her mother?"

"She never mentions her mother. Just her pappy and this Gracie person. I think Gracie either worked for them or was Ella's sister. Something tragic happened to the girl, so that's somehow tangled up in all of this."

"Our homestead was clear across town, on the opposite side of Juliet," Sybil said. "Back then, folks didn't just up and drive around for pleasure. It was the Great Depression, and my family didn't own a car. Banisha's house is five miles or so out of Naomi. Our paths didn't have much chance to cross."

"What about Banisha? What do we know about her?" Virgie asked.

"Not much. She and her husband moved here about two years ago. I'm thinking if the land belonged to her family," Granny Bert said, "they may have decided to move to the country."

"She doesn't strike me as a country girl. Have you seen what's in her pantry?" Wanda scoffed. "Nothing but health food and fancy imported brands. Ella says she can't even make a decent pot of red beans, and thinks cornbread comes from a box mix. No country girl worth her salt would commit such a travesty!"

"Quit snooping through her pantry," Virgie chided. "Now, if that's all, I'd better get Hank's pizza home to him. I don't normally indulge him that way, so he's looking forward to it."

"I think we all have our assignments for now," Granny Bert said. "Find out what we can about Ella's past, come up with a schedule for next week, and, for Heaven's sake, keep Ella away from that pin oak!"

18

"This is the *only* time you will ever hear these words come out of my mouth," Madison told Megan and the twins. "I want you to go to the concert down at the washout tonight."

Blake looked at his mother like she had lost her mind. "Wait. What did you just say?"

"You heard me. We need you to go to the concert. With stipulations, of course."

"Of course," Bethani said, rolling her eyes.

"Absolutely *no* alcohol," Madison stressed. "The last thing we need is for any of you to be arrested. Just go to the concert, act like zany kids having a great time at the beach, and have your phones on you at all times."

"Be alert," Brash added. "Watch for anyone who looks suspicious, especially if he's smoking a cigarette. Stay together and make sure you have an exit path."

"Let me get this straight," Megan said. Her eyes narrowed behind her trendy glasses. "You *want* us to go to a wild party down at the washout."

"Only because we trust you. Like your mother said, no alcohol. Stay together and stay safe. It wouldn't hurt to be a tad bit conspicuous."

"Oh, I can do conspicuous!" Blake assured him.

"I know you can, son. That's what we're counting on."

"Wear bright-colored shirts," Madison added. "Show us what you'll be wearing so we can pick you out of the crowd."

"I just now noticed, but both of you are wearing two shirts," Bethani said. Her eyes narrowed in suspicion. "Why?"

"So we can blend in with the party crowd, too. We'll ditch the top shirts and be ready for the concert."

Blake was incredulous. "You two are going to the concert? Now I know you've lost it!"

"If everything goes as planned, yes, we'll meet you at the concert."

"And if you don't?"

"If we don't," Brash said in a grave voice, "find a policeman or someone in authority. I know they'll have someone out there patrolling to make sure things don't get out of hand. Make up whatever story you have to but have them escort you back here."

"What if they want to take us to jail?"

"At least you'll be safe there."

"Hold on," Megan protested. "Is what you two are going to do be dangerous?"

"We're going to rescue Patty. If we fail, I'm not sure what will happen," Brash said honestly. "That's why it's important for us to know that you're safe."

"Then why are we going to the concert? I figured you'd make us stay here."

"Because if the second guy is watching the inn, trying to get a glimpse of Roberts, he'll see you three sneaking out and going to a party we would never approve of."

"But if you come to the party, too…"

"Even if he sees us, I don't think he'll recognize us. We'll look like a couple of over-aged groupies, trying to recapture their youth." Brash grinned, pulling his top shirt aside. He wore a psychedelic tee shirt that was two sizes too small. It boasted the faded emblem of a long-defunct rock group and showed off his chest and abs.

Megan's mouth fell open. "Da-ad! I can't believe you'd wear that in public."

"I know, right?"

"Mom?" Bethani asked. "What do you have on under there?"

Madison looked hesitant. "Maybe I shouldn't show you."

"Now you *have* to show us!" both girls cried.

Puffing her cheeks and blowing the air out slowly, Madison unbuttoned her overshirt.

"Mom! A cropped t-shirt?" Bethani cried in disbelief.

"Oh my gosh, Mama Maddy! You look great!"

"Great?" Blake demanded. "Great? That's my mom! She looks indecent!"

"If she wasn't your mother," Megan informed him with a droll look, "you'd think she looked hot. I didn't know you had a figure, Mama Maddy. You always dress so…"

"Old," Bethani supplied. "She dresses like Granny Bert."

"It's classic," Madison defended her wardrobe choices. She pulled her shirt closed and quickly buttoned it.

"I think you're definitely right, Daddy D." Bethani's eyes still looked dazed. "I'm not sure even we'd recognize you if we saw you in a crowd."

"You have your assignment," Brash said. "Don't take it lightly. Stay safe, stay sober, stay together, and stay vigilant."

Kronk—he didn't offer a last name—was, indeed, an interesting man.

He reminded Madison of Willie Nelson. Long, braided hair, scraggly beard, weathered skin. His voice was deeper than the legendary singer's and carried an indiscernible accent. She couldn't begin to guess his age.

He didn't speak much, preferring grunts and gestures. Amused, Madison thought he did a fine job of imitating the Indian characters on those old western movies she and Grandpa Joe used to watch.

He handed each of them a long, hand-carved walking stick and led them out to a battered old truck that had more scratches and dings than Granny Bert's favorite stew pot. They drove at an excruciatingly slow pace, ignoring the honks and rude gestures of other drivers along Highway 87.

After several miles, they turned onto a paved side street that led toward the ocean.

Instead of following it all the way to the beach, he pulled off the road and shifted the old truck into park.

"We walk the rest of the way. You have the backpack?" It was the longest string of words he had said to them so far.

"Right here," Brash confirmed, slinging it onto his back.

Kronk took the walking sticks from the bed of the truck and handed them over again. "Watch your step and stay quiet." He motioned for him to follow.

The concert was in full swing. Madison could hear the music and the crowd. Both sounded raucous. She prayed they had made the right decision in sending the kids there, but they were eighteen now, and she had to trust them. It was crucial to tonight's success.

The trek into the marshy area, the place that Sirenity called no-man's land, was slow and nerve racking. Tall grasses grew from the muddy ground, hiding deeper pockets of groundwater and who knows what else. They spooked more than a few herons, spoonbills, pelicans, and several coastal birds she couldn't identify. Her biggest fear was finding a snake or, far worse, an alligator.

She watched the way Kronk moved his stick in front of him in gentle strokes, quietly announcing his presence before taking his next step. She followed suit, finding the long stick also useful in keeping her balance.

Dusk was starting to fall, its effects more noticeable here in the marsh. The sounds of the concert grew fainter as they approached a small clearing. Kronk stopped, motioning for them to stay silent. With a gesture of his fingers, he directed them to stay in the tall grasses while he slipped around the perimeter of the clearing.

If Madison hadn't known he was there, she would have never seen his stealthy approach, nor his target. Only when he was upon it did she notice the rickety lean-to. Its weathered wood blended in with its surroundings, all but camouflaged to the unsuspecting eye.

After what seemed like an eternity, Kronk motioned for them to come forward.

Once upon the three-sided structure, Madison saw Patty. She was lying on her side, her hands and feet bound, with a dirty bandanna tied around her mouth. She was clearly frightened by the old man's presence, but when she saw the deCordovas, relief flooded into her eyes. Tears spilled down her cheeks.

The first thing Madison did was drop down on one knee and give the girl a long, motherly hug.

"It's okay, Patty. We're here now," Madison whispered. "And we're going to get you out of here."

Brash took a blanket from the backpack and wrapped it around the girl, while Kronk took a long-bladed knife and cut through her bindings.

"I'm going to take the gag off, but you mustn't talk," Brash whispered to her. "We're going to give you something to drink and eat, and then we're getting out of here. Do you think you can walk out on your own?"

She nodded.

"Try not to cry out. If your kidnapper comes back, he can't know you're free," Brash whispered, taking the gag off. Madison was waiting with a sports drink. The girl needed extra electrolytes.

They had taken the noisy foil wrapper off the energy bar at home and had it stored in a much quieter resealable plastic bag. Patty devoured it now in three bites.

"We need you to go with our friend Kronk," Madison told the girl, speaking close to her ear.

Patty darted her eye to the old man in fear.

"It's okay. He's a good man. He'll get you back safely. He's going to take you to his house, but Lindsey and her parents will be there. You'll be fine."

"Where...?" She looked back and forth between Madison and Brash, the question clear in her eyes.

"We need to stay here. We'll offer a diversion if the man comes back."

Brash quietly helped her to her feet, stabilizing her when her legs would have given way. Madison rubbed them briskly to get her circulation moving.

"You'll be okay, Patty," Brash assured her in his deep voice. It was just a whisper in her ear, but it gave her confidence. "Go with Kronk."

Madison took off her overshirt and placed it on the girl. Kronk took the backpack and two of the sticks, motioning for the girl to follow. With a single nod to the others, he silently wished them luck.

They gave him a few minutes head start before they left. Kronk had taken a different route than they had taken, one that would lead him and Patty directly back to the battered truck. Rivera would never suspect an ancient old clunker, all but crawling down the highway, to be the getaway car.

Confident the others were far enough away now, Madison giggled and stumbled from the lean-to, the blanket wrapped loosely around her shoulders. She gave no thought to snakes and alligators now. There was a bigger danger now; Riviera.

Brash had traded his overshirt for a ballcap in the backpack, which he now wore with the bill turned backwards. Sneaking away from the notoriously questionable structure, running through the grasses like two carefree lovers on a scandalous rendezvous, they hardly looked like the upstanding couple people in The Sisters knew and loved.

If Rivera were watching, he would think the girl had somehow gotten free, and the lovers had found the place empty. They were now taking their private little party back to the concert.

To keep up the charade, Brash and Madison rejoined the crowd with their arms above their head in what appeared to be wild abandon, dancing and singing along with the music. They waited until the third song to send a text to the kids and search for them among the crowd.

"There," Brash said, motioning discreetly with his head. "Blake kept up his end of the bargain. He is definitely being conspicuous."

Madison followed his gaze. Her son stood on top of the golf cart's roof, playing an 'air' guitar, and entertaining a small crowd of adoring females. Megan was his back-up singer, pantomiming the lyrics, while Bethani danced on the back of the cart.

"At least they did as we asked."

"And they appear to be safe, so that's all we can really ask for."

"That, and for Patty to get safely back to Kronk's."

Sirenity had suggested the arrangements. She reasoned that if Rivera were watching the inn, he would know the girl was inside. He had already invaded the rental where she was staying, so that option was no better. But no one would give a second glance to the old house half-hidden behind an untended hedge, bushy plants, and overgrown fronds. Kronk liked his privacy. In an area populated with vacation rentals and fancy beach houses, his rather shabby, unpainted house looked all but abandoned.

Sirenity would take the Lewis family there when she felt the coast was clear.

As for Samuel Roberts, he was no problem this evening. On the very real chance that he broke his promise and tried to save his daughter on his own, Sirenity had seen to it that he was locked inside his room. She enabled a safety mechanism on the locks, normally used only in the event of a lockdown. In today's world, a crazed lunatic with a knife or a gun couldn't be ruled out, and she needed a way to keep her guests safe.

After a few more songs, Madison and Brash danced their way toward the golf cart. Blake had already ended his 'show,' but he had autographed his fans' arms, hands, and, in one case, one very shapely waistline.

Texas state law mandated that fireworks could only be sold during the days preceding January first and July fourth, but most unincorporated areas allowed them to be enjoyed year-round. Bolivar was one of those places.

With a stash leftover from New Year's, Blake had brought along a few roman candles for his 'conspicuous' strategy. When he set off two and let them soar over the water, other partygoers followed suit.

While the crowd enjoyed the bonus show, the de-Rey family drove away on the golf cart.

"*Now* can you tell us why we were allowed to go to that concert tonight?" Blake asked.

"You had fun, didn't you?" his mother asked.

"Of course. It was a blast! And I got like a dozen phone numbers. But you normally don't encourage that sort of fun."

"And don't think we'll be making a habit of it," Brash was quick to say. "But tonight, we needed Rivera, the second stalker, to follow you."

"You used us for bait?" Megan asked incredulously. "Thanks, Dad. Way to make a girl feel loved."

"Did he bother you?"

"No," she admitted.

Bethani added, "I thought I saw him once,

following behind us on a dirt bike. Then I didn't see him after that."

"Because we set up *another* diversion for our diversion. Two, actually."

"Huh? You lost me at the first diversion," Blake told him.

"In case Rivera followed you, hoping to find Roberts doing the same thing, we had a decoy."

"Hold on. Why would Roberts be following us now? Patty's already been kidnapped."

"But maybe you were still looking for her, and you had an idea on where she might be. Roberts could have followed you. Or, maybe you were headed to meet Roberts to help him look. Either way, Rivera may have thought you were the key to finding Roberts, since he's not been seen anywhere else."

"A little farfetched," Blake grumbled, "but okay. What was the diversion?"

"If Rivera did follow you, he would have seen a man in the crowd who looked like Roberts and gotten diverted. By the time he found the man in the long coat and hat, he would realize his mistake."

"And if he didn't follow you," Madison said, "and waited for Roberts to leave the inn, he would have seen someone leave in a floppy brimmed hat and long-sleeved fishing shirt. If he followed the second decoy, he would have discovered the same mistake."

"Who did you get to do that? Did they have a death wish or something?" Megan mumbled.

"Kent Bergman and a buddy of his," Brash answered. "They jumped at the chance to have a little adventure. They're both ex-military and get a little bored with civilian life from time to time."

Blake turned to Madison. "And your scandalous outfit, young lady?" he wanted to know, eying his mother in mock outrage. "What do you have to say about that?"

"We're headed back to the inn, aren't we?" she asked, eyes twinkling. "I'd say it worked."

"Uh, guys," Bethani said, her voice quivering. "Not so fast. We may have a problem. A dirt bike is following us. And the driver looks determined to catch up with us."

"Don't panic. It could be anyone," Brash said, but he pressed the accelerator all the way to the floor.

The bike gained on them.

"Yeah, I don't think so," Blake said. "Dad, you gotta do something." He dropped the usual 'Daddy D' moniker, but Brash was too busy outrunning the dirt bike to appreciate it.

"Hold on, this might get rough," Brash warned. They were traveling at max speed, splashing through mud puddles, bouncing over bunched seaweed and random pieces of driftwood, bottoming out on rivulets cut through the sand and destroying abandoned sandcastles.

The dirt bike kept coming.

"What are we going to do?" Bethani cried.

"Yell at people to get out of the way," Brash said, honking his horn and frantically waving his arms. He deliberately drove through three different clusters of people still down on the beach, all who scattered in different directions. Their helter-skelter scramble slowed the bike following them, but not enough.

"He's still coming!" Megan yelled.

"I have an idea," Blake said. He dug through his backpack and found two roman candles and one rapid-fire, jumbo version of the firework.

He aimed one of the candles at the front of the bike. The colorful projectiles took the driver by surprise, but most of the shots soared over his head.

"Bad aim!" his twin criticized.

"I can see that." He tried again, aiming the second candle well in front of the advancing bike. The driver swerved and almost lost his balance, but he kept coming.

The jumbo stick was his last chance. Blake prepared the firework to launch.

"Hurry, Blake! He's getting closer!" his sisters both urged.

"Hold steady, Dad," he said, aiming the firework just so.

The timing was perfect. Even the surf cooperated. As the giant jumbo candle went off, temporarily blinding the driver with its brightness and forcing him to swerve the barrage of rapid-fire shots, the tide rushed in. The driver lost his balance, teetered for a moment as the last of the fireworks rained down on him, and lost the fight against nature. The tide wasn't strong enough to carry him off to sea, but it was enough to bring down his bike.

"Washout!" Blake yelled in victory.

Brash drove back to the Mermaid's Retreat at top speed.

19

Sirenity had disengaged the safety feature on Roberts' door so he could open it when Brash knocked.

Once inside, Brash told the worried father two all-important words. "She's safe."

"Oh, thank God!" Roberts collapsed on the small sofa, unabashed tears of relief rolling down his scarred face. "Can I see her? Is she here?"

"She's somewhere safe," Brash assured him. "She needs her rest tonight. Tomorrow, we'll see about letting you meet your daughter."

"I need to meet her. I need to explain to her why I've been away all these years. I—I need to tell her how much I love her."

"I know that, and I do understand. I do. I'm a father, too, you know. But even though she's safe for tonight, we need to keep her that way. And we need to keep you safe, too. Getting you both out of here won't be easy. And whether you like it or not, it's time to call in the cops."

"No! I don't trust them. Tar-Go does business

here. Do you realize how many people in this area depend on Tar-Go Chemical for a paycheck? If not directly, indirectly. Anybody can be bought. Everyone has a price."

"Not everyone," Brash said with conviction.

"Maybe not in dollar figures," Roberts said. "But wouldn't you do anything to keep your family safe?"

"Of course."

"Then that's your price. The safety of your family."

Brash let out a heavy breath. The man had a point.

After giving the situation some thought, he said, "We'll call the DA's office. He has a price tag, too. The price of winning. The price of his career. He's been after Tar-Go for years. He's not going to risk losing them now, not when he's this close."

Roberts didn't immediately object, which Brash took as a good sign. "Is Loretta down here?" he asked after a moment.

"No. She doesn't know about any of this. The Lewises didn't want her driving down here on her own." His mouth set in a grim line. "I was going to send a car for her tomorrow, but maybe it's best if she didn't come. Rivera won't take being outsmarted lying down."

"Then I need you to have someone go to her house tonight and make sure she's safe. They'll go after my wife next."

"I've already considered that. I know a guy with a private security business. I took the liberty of asking him to watch the house tonight. He won't be pulled away on an official call like a police officer might be, but if you keep him on after tonight, his services won't come cheap."

"I'll pay it."

Brash nodded and stood to leave. "Let me make a call."

Roberts' voice stopped him at the door. "deCordova?"

"Yeah?"

"Thank you. I don't know how I'll ever repay you."

"By keeping your family safe—yourself safe—and testifying in that courtroom."

"What happens after that? What will keep them from coming after me and my family, even if a jury finds them negligent?"

"That's not up to me. The DA will talk to you about that."

"She's really safe?" Bethani asked Brash when he returned. Everyone was gathered in the common room of their suite, reliving the day's events.

The first thing Madison had done was change into dry pants and, most importantly, a more modest top. A pair of comfy pajamas had filled both needs just right.

"She's really safe," Brash confirmed, dropping onto the couch between the two girls. "At least for tonight, anyway. So, I suggest we all get a good night's rest. We may have a long day in store for us tomorrow."

"What do you mean, for tonight?" Blake questioned from where he lounged on the other sofa beside his mother. "She's still not out of danger?"

"I hope she is, but it's too soon to say. I'm confident Rivera won't find her at Kronk's house, but there's still the matter of getting her back home safely. Going back to their rental isn't an option. She needs to leave the island."

"Who is this Kronk character, anyway?"

"A real character, that's for sure," his mother commented. "Sirenity says he's taken her under his wing and looks out for her. She trusts him explicitly, so that's good enough for us."

"What a weird name. Is it a nickname?" Blake asked.

"Who knows? That's how she introduced him. No last name, just Kronk."

"That's what they used to call the Karankawa Indians." Bethani nodded. "They once inhabited the coastal plains of Texas but are now extinct."

"Not according to Kronk. He claims to be a direct descendant of the tribe, which he insists didn't die out. He said they just mingled with other tribes in order to survive."

"Hmm. I'll have to check that out," Bethani mused.

Before her history-loving sister and best friend could launch into another lesson on early Texas, Megan pointed out a flaw in her father's logic. "If she's not safe at the rental house, her dorm room won't be much better. They have to know that's where she lives."

"The dorm itself may be," Brash countered. "They have security measures in place. But the campus is more open. And getting to and from the campus safely will be a problem, too. She'll need around-the-clock protection, at least until her father testifies in court."

Blake whistled lowly. "This is really heavy stuff."

"It is. You kids did great tonight, but there's nothing more you can do for now. You may as well get some rest."

"What about you two?"

"I have a phone call I need to make," Brash said, "but then I think I'll take my own advice. It's been a long day."

Once the kids were in their bedrooms, and the couple crawled into their own bed, Madison asked her husband, "What happens now? How *will* Patty get back to Huntsville? Or will she go home to Lufkin?"

"Where she goes after this isn't our call. But I did tell Roberts I would help get her off the peninsula."

"How? Get the Galveston County Sheriff's Department to help?"

"That was my suggestion, but Roberts pointed out that Tar-Go has a lot of influence down here. They're responsible for a lot of jobs, so the economy depends on them. He's afraid they can buy loyalty, even from the law. I hate to say it, but he's not wrong."

"What do you propose?"

"I suggested the DA's office. Roberts is their witness. He escaped the safe house they had him stashed in originally, so I'm sure they'd feel better knowing he was back under their thumb. They'd probably accept Patty and her mother, as well, just to keep Roberts happy."

"Now, to get the DA's detectives here, or Patty there."

"Right. Which we'll tackle tomorrow. I wasn't joking when I said this has been a long day."

"What a vacation, huh?" Madison sighed, turning off her bedside lamp. "I can't believe we only have one more night here."

"I guess we can never get away from our jobs completely," he admitted. "Snooping just seems to be in your blood."

She snuggled against his side. "And coming to the rescue seems to be in yours."

Brash was up early, concocting a plan with the DA's office. He explained how Rivera was there, keeping close tabs on Roberts, and how the man had kidnapped Patty. He warned that extricating either of them from Bolivar would be tricky.

They came up with a multi-faceted plan, one Brash felt confident might just work.

First, Lindsey and her parents left Kronk's house at dawn, taking a convoluted path back to their beach house, should Rivera be watching for their arrival. They left Patty with her duffel bag and a promise to see her soon.

Meanwhile, Brash once again recruited Kent's help.

With Patty dressed in borrowed clothes, she easily passed as a boy. Kronk and his battered old truck delivered her to Kent's house along the canal, where she was told Brash would meet her. Her cell phone was still in her kidnapper's possession, leaving the girl feeling bereft and disconnected, among so many other things.

Sirenity came up with the next phase of the plan. She had a delivery coming from a food supplier that morning, and she knew the driver well enough to beg a favor. He had an extra uniform in the truck and agreed to temporarily swap shirts with Brash. Soon, both Brash and Roberts walked out to the truck in the borrowed clothes and crawled inside. No one gave them a second glance as they left the inn, made another stop at a nearby restaurant, and ended up at Kent's door.

"Kent, I can't tell you how much I appreciate all your help," Brash said, shaking his friend's hand in greeting.

"Are you kidding me?" the other man grinned. "I haven't had so much fun since I accidentally blew up a silt reef out by Goat Island!"

"Remind me to never introduce you to Maddy's grandmother. The two of you could stir up a whole heap of trouble."

"Is that the infamous Granny Bert? I remember her from the TV show."

"We'd rather forget *Home Again*, if it's all the

same to you," he said with a grimace. "How's Patty?"

"My daughter has her occupied at the moment, bombarding her with questions about college. She wants to go to Sam when she graduates."

"Thanks, again, for letting her come over. And for letting us use your house for a very special reunion."

"Happy to do it. Where's your friend?"

"Waiting for me to break the ice with Patty. Mind keeping him company? He's a little antsy."

"Understandable."

"Oh, and just to give you a head's up. He has some significant scarring."

"Who doesn't?" Kent pulled his collar aside, showing an ugly scar that started at his collarbone and traveled beneath his shirt. "Souvenir for serving my country."

"Thanks, buddy. Both for the service and for the favor. I owe you big."

"Just get in there and talk to the girl," Kent said gruffly.

When Patty saw Brash's familiar face, she ran to him and threw herself into his arms. "Thank you for coming! I've been so scared. What's going on? No one will tell me anything!"

After a warm hug, Brash led her to the sofa. "Let's sit down, and I'll try to clear some things up. I have a lot to tell you."

"Okay."

"Your friends tell me you never really talk about your dad. What do you know about him?"

The young woman picked at her nail.

"Nothing, really. My mom says he's probably dead. And that if he's not, she doesn't want to know about it. He disappeared a long time ago, and he's never tried to contact either one of us. She says we're better off without him."

"Have you ever heard of a company called Tar-Go Chemical?"

The change of subject threw her, but she answered readily enough. "Sure. Who hasn't? Not just because of their commercials, but chemistry is sort of my thing. I hear they offer a program at Sam, but I haven't had a chance to check into yet. Why do you ask?"

"Seventeen years ago, one of their top and most brilliant chemists discovered a major flaw at one of their oil refineries. He went to leadership and explained the problem. He even offered a way to rectify the situation, but they ignored him."

"Why would they do that? That could have major consequences."

"Which is what he told them, but they said implementing the changes would be too costly. They chose to ignore him."

"What happened?"

"He wound up blowing the whistle, reporting them to the Texas Railroad Commission, who regulates the refineries and most of the oil industry."

"Good for him! Did they see reason and fix the error?"

"Unfortunately, no. Before any further action could be taken, there was an explosion at the refinery."

"That's horrible!" Patty cried, putting her hands over her mouth. "Was anyone killed?"

"Sadly, yes. Many people lost their lives that day, although not all of those died. Not in the literal sense. But the ones with the worst injuries lost their lives as they knew it. They were emotionally, physically, and mentally scarred, not unlike soldiers who come back from combat or people who have other traumatic injuries."

"That's awful," she repeated. "Those poor people!"

"The whistle blower, the chemist who was just trying to do the right thing and prevent what eventually happened, was one of those people. He was gravely injured, and for a while, he lost his memory. It took years before everything came back to him."

"That poor, brave man," she said sympathetically. "I can't imagine what he must have gone through."

"He still bears the physical scars from that day. Some are graphic and almost painful to look at."

"Imagine how they must feel!"

"His emotional scars are even worse. He lost everything. His career. His wife. His child. Even his identity. It took a long time before he remembered his name was Samuel Roberts."

Patty grew very still. "That—That was my father's name. I saw it on my birth certificate."

Brash covered her hand with his. In a gentle voice, he told her, "That's because that brilliant chemist—that man who tried to do the right thing by alerting the authorities—is your father, Patty."

"My f—father?"

"Yes. And he'd like to meet you. But there's still a lot you don't know, and I need to tell you that before you decide whether or not you'd like to meet him."

Her eyes clouded with doubt. "You said he was hurt? That he lost his memory?"

"Yes, that's right."

Her voice hardened. "But even when he remembered who he was, he didn't contact us."

"That's what I want to explain to you."

"What's there to explain? He chose to ignore us! He let me grow up without a father. He let my mother work two jobs, with little time for me or for herself, just to make ends meet." She crossed her arms across her chest in a defensive gesture. "No. I don't need to decide. I know right now I don't want to meet him. He rejected us all those years, so I'm rejecting him now."

"It's not that simple, Patty. He wasn't rejecting you. He was trying to protect you."

"Protect me? From what? His scars?" she asked in scorn.

"No. Although I do imagine *he* needs protection from them sometimes," he said softly. "They're bad. Some people can't see beyond them to see the man behind them."

"But we were his family! My mom loved him. And—And I did, too. I have these vague memories of him..." She angrily pushed away a tear. "Why are you telling me all this? To make me feel sorry for him?"

"Sympathy is the last thing he wants from you. All he wants is to meet you and to tell you his side of the story."

"Well, I don't want to meet him," she said. She sounded more like a stubborn child than a conscientious young adult. "I don't care what his story is."

"Are you sure about that? Because that man has given up his entire life to keep you safe."

"Again, from what? An ugly face? Looks don't matter to me," she insists. "It's what's inside a person that matters."

"I'm glad you feel that way. Because inside that man is a heart of gold. Think about the risks he took, turning in a major conglomerate like Tar-Go Chemical. He knew it would cost him his job. Possibly his reputation as a chemist. But he didn't care because he valued human life more than he did material things. And even though he wanted more than anything to be reunited with his wife and daughter, he stayed away because it was the only way he knew to keep you both safe."

He saw the argument brewing on her lips. "He knew his life was in danger," Brash rushed on before she could say anything. "He didn't want to put yours in danger, too."

"Why—Why was his life in danger?"

"He had turned them in once already. Tar-Go managed to deflect the blame, but they were swamped with lawsuits. The only person who could prove they were at fault was your father. And once they realized he was alive and could testify against them, they knew they had to get rid of him."

"Rid of him. As in—" She couldn't bring herself to say the words.

"In whatever way it took," Brash confirmed. "He refused to bring that danger to his family's doorstep."

"So, he just... stayed away?"

"What else could he do? After seventeen long years, the case is finally going to trial, thanks in large part to your father. He has evidence against the company, and he plans to expose it, and them, at a very crucial trial set for next month."

"I still don't understand why..."

"Then let him explain it to you. Please, Patty. After all this, don't you at least think you should hear him out?"

The girl looked torn. "I—I guess," she said. "But why is he here? Why now?"

"He'll explain that, too."

She gasped with sudden insight. "Is that why I was kidnapped? It was the people trying to hurt him?"

"They knew the best way to keep him quiet was to threaten his family. But this is his story to tell, not mine. Will you hear him out? Will you meet your father?"

Patty closed her eyes as tears streamed down her face. "Yes," she said in a whisper.

"I'll let you two have some time alone, but I'll be close by if you need me."

"Th—Thank you."

"Of course."

He sent a quick text and stayed with Patty until her father knocked at the door, ready for their long-awaited reunion.

20

Brash was already gone that morning, off to complete this last all-important phase of their mission. Madison anxiously waited for word on how the reunion had gone between Patty and her long-lost father.

She drank her coffee on the deck, soaking up the sounds of the ocean and the tang of its fresh, salty air. She wished she could bottle this feeling and take it back to The Sisters with her.

It was hard to believe their vacation was almost over. Tomorrow, they would check out and go back to the real world. She wasn't ready to face the grind of everyday life just yet or the ticking clock that counted down the days until her babies graduated. Life moved too fast. Even this vacation hadn't been the relaxing, stress-free break they had anticipated. She still needed time to unwind.

Ready for her second cup of coffee, she went inside to brew another cup in the Keurig. Once the kids were up and among the living, they would go down and eat breakfast together. She wasn't ready to let them out of her sight just yet. Not with Rivera still on the loose, Brash gone, and Roberts and Patty's safety still hanging in the balance.

She was startled when someone knocked on their door. Before she reached it, a woman's voice called out in an urgent whisper, "Mrs. deCordova? I need to speak with you. It's urgent."

Madison didn't recognize the voice. "Who is it?" she asked cautiously. She looked through the peephole and thought it might the woman who had a bad habit of listening in on their conversations. The one here celebrating her wedding anniversary.

"Doniece Rae," she said. "My husband and I are guests here at the inn."

"I'll be down for breakfast soon. Can it wait?"

"No. No, this urgent!" she hissed. "It—It's about your husband."

A dozen thoughts flew through Madison's head, none of them good. She cautiously opened the door enough to peer out at her unexpected visitor.

"Is Brash all right? Is he hurt?"

"No, not yet."

Heart hammering, Madison asked, "What happened? Is he in danger?"

A man stepped from behind Doniece Rae and pushed both their ways inside the suite.

Madison was too stunned—and too worried about Brash—to protest the invasion. "Is Brash in danger?" she repeated.

"He will be," the man said in a low, threatening voice, "if you don't do exactly as I say."

"What—What is this?" Madison asked, taking

a step backward. It was in direct contrast to her words. She pointed to the door and asserted, "I think you both should leave."

"I think not," the man said. He kicked the door shut so that his companion could engage the deadlock.

"What are you doing?" Madison cried. "Who are you?"

"You can call us the Raes," he replied. "Doniece and Johnny Rae were… kind enough… to lend us their identities for the week." The way he said the words didn't bode well for the unknown couple. The look in his eyes didn't bode well for Madison and her children.

"There's no reason for anyone to get hurt," his 'wife' said. Madison doubted they were actually married.

"You heard her," the man said. "As long as you do as I say, you and your kids are safe."

The kids! Madison needed to get a message to them, so they wouldn't come out of their rooms. Neither bedroom had access to the deck, but Blake was agile. Could he climb out a window, somehow swing over to their deck, and… and, what? There were no stairs off their balcony, and they were at least twelve feet off the lower deck. Jumping would be too dangerous.

"Give me your phone," the man demanded.

"I don't have it. I left it on the deck," Madison lied.

"What's that bulge in your pocket?"

"None of your business."

His stare was cold and somehow threatening. "Do you want me to search you?" To help persuade her, he pulled aside the Hawaiian shirt he wore over a white tee. A gun was tucked into the waistband of his shorts.

"Now," he said, assuming the issue was settled. He held out his hand, palm up. "That phone."

Madison sighed and handed it over. She'd have to get a message to Brash—and the kids—some other way.

"Where's your husband?" Rae asked.

"I don't know."

"You're lying."

"No, I'm not. I don't know where he is." It was true. He could be enroute back to the inn. He could still be at Kent's. She didn't know his whereabouts for certain.

"Guess."

"Walking on the beach? Fishing? Making a donut run? I don't know for sure."

"Not good enough." He took the gun from his waistband and waved it at her.

Madison lifted her chin and told him stubbornly, "Waving the gun at me won't give me special powers. I don't have a crystal ball, so I don't know where he is."

"Then call him."

"You have my phone."

"Then I'll text him on your behalf. Here, *Doniece*." He sneered as he said the name and handed it to the other woman. "Find his name and send him a text."

Finding the conversation thread, her fingers poised over the keyboard. "What am I saying?"

"Tell him to bring Roberts back to the inn. It's urgent. Matter of life and death."

Madison forced herself to look confused. "Roberts? Who's Roberts?"

"You know who Roberts is! And now it's up to you to persuade your husband to bring him here."

"Do you mean the man smoking the cigarette? The one who's been following my children and their friends?"

"That's Rivera, and you know it. I'm talking about the man he's been following. The one staying at the end of the hall."

"I thought his name was Smith."

"Stop playing stupid. It's not a good look on you."

The woman was busy typing something on Madison's phone. When it binged, Rae asked sharply, "What's he say?"

Before she could answer, Bethani stumbled sleepily into the room, looking down at her phone's screen. "What's going on, Mom? What's so urgent that we have to come in—" She stopped short when she saw the other people in the room and the gun the man held. "Hey! What's going on?"

"Come over here, Beth," Madison said as calmly as she could muster. She motioned for her daughter to get behind her.

"What...? Who...?"

"I don't know, sweetie. Just stay calm."

"Mo-om!" Blake complained as he staggered

into the common room. "I thought we were sleeping in!"

The man answered his question, "Change of plans," he said. He waved the gun, motioning for Blake to join the others.

"You're the couple staying here," Blake said, recognizing them. "Why are you in here, and why do you have a gun? What's going on?"

"Not your concern. Just do what we say. Where's the other one?"

Madison feigned innocence. "The other what?"

"The other girl. The one with the brunette hair and the glasses."

Bethani's voice was pitched higher than normal, indicating her nervousness. As her mother of eighteen years, Madison also knew it could mean she was hiding something. "Y—Yeah, Mom, where is Megan?"

Madison looked at her sharply, deciding if it was a ruse or something to be concerned about. "You don't know?"

"She, uh, got up early," the young woman stammered. "Something about... walking on the beach."

Madison knew better than to believe her daughter, but she hoped the others did. She and the kids had talked last night, about how important it was to stick together today. Megan wasn't irresponsible enough to wander off on her own.

The twins stood close together. Bethani had her hands behind her back, wearing her best look of innocence. Blake stood slightly in front of her, perhaps to defend her, perhaps to hide the phone in her hands.

"Your husband hasn't answered," Doniece broke in. "What's wrong?"

"How would I know?" Madison asked irritably. "Maybe he and Megan are down on the beach together, having a heart to heart. I told you I don't have a crystal ball."

"And I told you," the man said, stepping close enough to loom over her, "you'd better find one, because we're not playing around here. We need Roberts!"

"Why? So he can't testify against Tar-Go?" she asked smugly. "You two are some of their goons, too, aren't you?"

"I thought you didn't know who Roberts was."

Madison shrugged. "My memory came back to me."

"Then you'd better remember where your husband and other daughter are, too, before my finger slips off this trigger."

"So, you and Rivera were working together, spying on Roberts? How did you know he would be here at the inn? And where are the real Raes?" The longer she stalled, asking questions she truly wanted answers to, the longer it gave Megan to do whatever it was she had planned. Most likely with Bethani's help.

More than once, the school administrators had called Madison to say that her daughter was being discipled for violating the rules of cell phone usage. Bethani was somewhat of an expert at texting. It always amazed Madison how her daughter's fingers flew over the keyboard, even without watching what she did. She had perfected typing behind her back so the teachers wouldn't catch her. Madison assumed that was what she had done this time. She had probably shot off a text to Megan, perhaps even Brash, using their secret code word for danger: Gravy.

Blake, of course, had come up with the name. Gravy, he reasoned, covered just about anything, and made any food, other than sweets, taste better. An emergency wasn't sweet, so the word fit. It had become their family's code for danger. Send help. Approach with care. Don't ask questions, just do it.

Gravy covered it all.

"You ask a lot of questions," the woman calling herself Doniece complained.

"I think I have a right to know why you're here, threatening my family."

"Fine. We had a tap on Roberts' phone. Knew he booked a room here. We found out who else was here for the w—'"

"You hacked her reservation system?" Madison protested.

"What?" 'Johnny' scoffed. "It's illegal? Unethical? You really think that matters to our employer?"

"So what happened to the real Raes?" she asked.

Doniece waved her hand dismissively. "Out of the picture."

Madison didn't want to know if she meant temporarily or permanently. She hoped for the former.

Johnny was tired of the distractions. "Look. None of that matters. What matters is that we get Roberts. Do whatever you have to do, but make it happen."

"I assume you checked Roberts' room?"

Doniece glared at her. "Oh, gee, why didn't we think of that?"

"Has my husband answered yet?"

The other woman glanced at the phone. "Not yet."

"Then I don't know what to do," Madison said with a shrug.

"You're going to have to call him," her accomplice decided. "I'll hold the phone while you talk. No funny business. I'll have it on speaker phone."

The call went to voicemail, so she left him a coded message.

"Brash! I was in the suite, making *gravy,* when that young couple burst in, demanding to see Roberts. They want you to bring him here."

From behind her, Blake yelled, "They have a gun!"

"Shut up!" the man snarled. He didn't bother with the ruse after that. He didn't need Madison's cooperation to make a threat. "DeCordova," he said into the phone, "you have thirty minutes to bring us Roberts, or we start shooting your family. Your choice."

"Mom!" Bethani whispered urgently. "What are we going to do?"

"I'll tell you what you're going to do." Once again, the man answered before Madison could, "You're going to sit down, shut up, and do what we say."

Bethani sank onto the sofa, hiding her phone between the cushions and making a show of holding her brother's hand for support. Madison perched on the armrest, hoping to put a barrier between her children and the couple holding them at gunpoint.

Where was Brash? Had he heard the message?

And where was Megan? Madison could only pray the girl didn't do anything stupidly brave.

Helpful, yes.

Stupid, no.

Seeing her sister's text while in the bathroom, Megan knew there was a problem. She could hear voices coming from the common room, and she didn't recognize all of them. The man's voice held a gruff, intimidating edge.

She looked around for a way to defend her family. Nothing.

She had three choices.

Text her father and take a chance on the other man finding her and dragging her in with the others, to do who knew what to them.

Attempt an escape and go for help.

Or create a diversion and try to save her family herself.

None were optimal, but she was running out of time to decide. Any moment now, the couple outside would realize they were short a kid and come looking for her.

Hiding in closets and under the bed were too cliche. She had to think of something more creative.

The jack-and-jill bath connected the two bedrooms. She slipped into Blake's room, scrunched her nose at its trademark *boy funk*, and avoided the open door into the common room. A quick search through his duffel bag produced more fireworks and a butane lighter.

Forgive me, Miss Sirenity, she said silently, *for what I'm about to do.*

She sent her stepmother and siblings a quick one-word text. *Spuds.* It went with gravy and was code for 'be ready.' Even if the bad people had confiscated their phones, with any luck, they had forgotten about smart watches.

Bethani must have seen hers. She suddenly yelled, "Oh, my gosh! Is that a *snake*?"

She must have pointed toward the door, because Megan saw the woman standing beside it whirl around with a cry of surprise. It gave Megan the perfect chance to light the string of firecrackers and lay them quietly outside the bedroom door. Before they detonated, she rolled two M-2 firecrackers into the room. The mega-sized firecrackers sounded like gunshots as one exploded in front of the woman, the other behind a chair.

Megan didn't wait to see if the man had seen her. She scampered through the bathroom and into their adjoining bedroom as the string of firecrackers went off.

The man predictably whirled toward the noise, aiming his gun in reflex. The woman screamed and fumbled with the door locks, determined to escape.

Madison was the first one off the couch, but Blake and Beth weren't far behind. They rushed the man with the gun, pushing him to the floor. The pistol skittered and slid across the room.

Too nervous to have success with the locks, the woman was still at the door. Megan saw her turn back to see what the commotion was, realized her partner was incapacitated, and let her eyes travel to the gun.

Before the woman could move to pick it up, Megan rushed into the room, grabbed the first heavy object she saw—a lovely glass seagull statuette—and hurled it with all her might. The seagull slammed against the door and shattered into a thousand pieces. She couldn't worry about that now. She was diving for the gun, determined to reach it before the woman did.

She dropped, rolled, and came upright with the gun held exactly the way she had learned. "Stop!" She summoned a voice of authority as she said, "Empty your pockets. If you have a weapon, I swear I'll shoot you before you can use it. I'm a distinguished marksman in handgun competition. Don't think I don't know how to use this."

Over her shoulder, never taking her eyes off the woman, Megan asked her family, "Y'all okay over there?"

"Yes," Mama Maddy said, but she sounded short of breath. Even though there were three of them, the man was probably stronger.

In truth, it felt to Madison like she was wrestling an octopus. It reminded her of when the twins were little, and she had to battle four arms and four legs just to get them settled into bed.

Blake had both of the man's arms bent at an awkward angle behind his back. "Sorry to do this, Mom," he said, releasing his hold on one arm just long enough to grab her abandoned cup from the nearby end table. The coffee was long cold, but the cup was heavy. He cracked it as hard as he could across the man's head, and suddenly, their octopus went lax.

"Ohmygosh, did you kill him?" his sister cried in horror.

"Does it matter? He planned to kill us," Blake snapped. Despite his gruff reply, he looked rattled at the prospect.

"Find something to tie him with," Megan instructed. "Then tie this one up." She indicated the woman.

"I guess the gun makes you the boss?" he grumbled but ran to his bedroom to find his braided, heavy gauge fishing line to do the honors.

Moments later, Sirenity and Brash burst into the room and found the amusing sight. The twins sat atop the back of a bound man, still out cold, while Madison talked with 9-1-1, using hand gestures and exact details. Megan stood nearby holding a gun, switching her sharp gaze between the prone man and a glaring woman sitting on the bar stool, her own hands and feet tied to its metal railings. A dirty sock was stuffed into her mouth.

Judging from the smell of it, Brash assumed the sock was Blake's special touch.

21

"I can't believe it's time to say goodbye," Madison told their hostess with a long hug the next morning.

"I know. It's been an eventful week, hasn't it?" Sirenity laughed.

"Too much so! I don't know how things went so wrong with that quiet, peaceful vacation we had planned, but I thank you so much for all your help."

"Thank *you*, all of you, for saving poor Patty. And for saving her father, as well."

"I suppose this is where you say, 'I told you so,'" Madison admitted.

"About what?"

"You predicted that Mr. 'Smith' was here because he had lost something, and because he wanted to make amends. You turned out to be exactly right."

"But even I never dreamed that something was his daughter! That came completely out of the blue."

"Is that a play on words?" Madison teased.

"Your name is Sirenity *Blue*."

"Pure coincidence," she claimed, palms up. "I missed this one."

"Missed what?" Brash asked, coming back from loading the last of their bags into the Expedition. "Another damage we incurred? Like I said, ring it up and charge it to my card. I'm afraid our kids did quite a number on our room."

"Nonsense. The figurine and bowl can be replaced. Even the floor wasn't badly scared from the firecrackers. All worth it, I can assure you, to catch the fake Mr. and Mrs. Rae."

"Any update on the real couple's condition?"

As soon as Madison told her about the duplicity, Sirenity had called their number. When no one answered, she called the local police and asked them to do a welfare check. They found the couple roughed up, bound, and gagged, but otherwise healthy.

"A night in the hospital for observation, and they've both been released. They should be fine," Sirenity was happy to report.

"That's good. And their impostors spent the first of many nights yet to come behind bars," Brash supplied.

"Rivera?" Sirenity asked.

"They caught him at the border, trying to sneak back into Mexico."

"At least Samuel Roberts and his family are under protective custody. That's comforting to know."

"Again," Madison said, "in large part thanks to

you."

"And you. Your entire family is amazing. You work together like a well-tuned orchestra."

Madison winced. "I hate to admit it, but we've had practice. This isn't our first 'case' to work."

"All in a day's work for you, I suppose, but much too stressful for me!" Sirenity laughed.

"Says the woman who runs this place by herself," Brash said. "You're a hero in your own right."

After more goodbyes, Brash went out to gather the teens, who were taking last-minute selfies with the ocean as their backdrop.

"You know, Madison," Sirenity said with a thoughtful expression on her face. "What I told you about myself and my talent to… interpret people and their emotions—"

When she paused, Madison squeezed her arm. "I promise not to doubt you again."

"That's good to hear, but that wasn't what I wanted to say. I wanted to point out that you and I aren't all that different in that regard. As a detective, even if you're an amateur one, you read people, too. You act on your instincts."

"You're right. Brash always says to listen to my gut instincts." Madison hazel eyes twinkled. "Genny and I have an imaginary business we call Snoop 'n Soup. I guess the two of us could open Snoop 'n Snooze." She wiggled her eyebrows. "What do you say? Want to be imaginary partners?"

"Imaginary is about the only way I could do it," Sirenity said. "I'm not cut out for danger."

"I'll draw up the imaginary documents, and we'll sign them the next time I come."

"Which had better not be as long as the last time," Sirenity chastised.

"I'd like to promise it won't be, but with the dreaded month of May coming up..."

Sirenity looked surprised. "Dreaded? May's a lovely time of year."

"Not when you have all three of your babies graduating at the same time and are facing empty-nest syndrome."

"All the more reason for you to come back this fall!"

"I'm going to pretend they'll all come home every weekend, and I'll be too busy, but we both know that's dreaming on my part," Madison sighed.

The Klintworth family came tromping down the stairs, their mother cautioning her boys not to run.

"I know you have other guests to check out, and we have a long drive ahead of us," Madison said. "Keep in touch, my friend. And thank you again for everything."

"And thank *you* for a very interesting week here on Bolivar!"

On the way back to The Sisters, the de-Reys reviewed their favorite parts of the week.

"The beach, of course. And the sunshine," Bethani said. "I even got started on my summer tan."

"The sunshine was great," Megan agreed. "I

could have done without the secrets."

"The fireworks ended up being pretty cool," Blake said. "And to think. Everyone made fun of me for keeping them and bringing them with us."

"Okay, you may now hoard fireworks to your heart's content," Megan granted him permission. "They came in rather handy, if I do say so myself."

"Let's not make a habit of setting them off in hotel rooms or at people on the beach," Madison said. "This was a one-time exception."

"At least Sirenity was cool about it," Megan said.

"Yeah, yeah," Blake replied to them both. His tone was dismissive.

"And that goes for dorm rooms, too, young man!" she thought to add.

A few miles down the road, Bethani admitted, "As much fun as I had this week—other than the whole Patty getting kidnapped, being chased by a crazed man on a motor bike, and then the being held at gunpoint thing—I sort of missed home. I wonder what Granny Bert's been doing all week without us."

"Actually, she and the girls—and yes, I use the term loosely, and yes, it also includes Derron—took on a case this week. They're sitting for Banisha Vickers' mom until she finds a new rest home to live in."

"'Isn't Mrs. Vickers that lady who works at Uncle Joe Glenn's bank?" Bethani asked.

"That's the one."

"They live a few miles out of Naomi," Blake recalled. "They hired *Marvin Gardens* to clean up the yard and plant all new sod when they renovated that rundown old house. They've finished it now, and it looks great, but you should have seen it when we first went out there!"

Out of curiosity, Megan asked, "What was wrong with her mother's old rest home?"

"No clue," Madison answered. "But she has a habit of being kicked out of them, so I think the trouble is with her, not them."

"And you turned her loose with Granny Bert for the week?" Blake questioned her judgment as he gave her a look of horror. "They may have blown up the bank by now!"

"First of all, you know Granny Bert's son owns Juliet Bank and Trust. Second of all… well, maybe there's not a second of all, but the first reason works."

"There's a bank across the tracks in Naomi. Which your arch enemy Barry Redmond ran until you sent him to jail."

Madison sent a nervous, sideways look at her husband. "You haven't heard anything about a recent plot to blow up the First State Bank of Naomi, have you?"

"Well, I did give my officers explicit instructions not to bother me this week with trivial matters," he admitted. "But I think something like that would warrant mentioning, so I think we're good."

"I hope so." Madison still nibbled on her lip.

"Thanks, son." Brash gave Blake 'the eye' through the mirror. "Now you've made your mother worry."

"Hey. It's a legitimate worry," he defended himself. "At least Granny Bert hasn't been firing her shotgun at people this week, or they would have called you."

"Eh, maybe not. It's only loaded with rock salt, and usually whoever she's shooting at deserves it. My officers could have overlooked it."

"That's true. But obviously, Derron didn't take his hairdresser boyfriend back, or his hair would be psychedelic again and causing fender benders from everyone pointing at him."

"And," Bethani pitched in, trying to look at the bright side of things, "Miss Wanda hasn't made a scene on half-price Margarita Night down at *Montelongo's*, or been taken to *Texas General* ER for a mistaken heart attack. Laurel would have called you if she had been admitted."

Madison hadn't heard from her friend lately, emergency department head nurse Laurel Benson at the College Station hospital. She made a mental note to check in with her. Better yet, they should invite her and Cade Resnick for supper one night. Genny and Cutter could come, too. Just the six of them, catching up on their busy lives.

"And Miss Virgie isn't pulling secret husbands out of the woodwork, having their nephews hire you to ghost-proof their houses for them," Megan said.

"Come to think of it, Miss Sybil is the only one who doesn't cause a stir," Bethani pointed out. "How did she ever become friends with them?"

"She and Granny Bert have been best friends

since they were girls. I've heard about some of their exploits when they were younger, but for the most part, Miss Sybil has a calming effect on your great-grandmother. Like Grandpa Joe did before he passed away."

"I don't know about that," Blake argued. "I remember some of the things she used to do when we were little. That was one of the reasons Grandmother Annette didn't like us visiting, much less moving in with her. She said Granny Bert was a bad influence on us."

"She may have had a point, but Annette has mellowed somewhat over the latest couple of years. She'd never admit it, but I think she secretly likes Granny Bert. At the very least, she admires her spunk."

"Who doesn't?" Megan marveled. "I want to *be* Granny Bert when I'm eighty years old!"

"Get that notion out of your head, young lady, or I'll come back to haunt you," her father threatened. "And don't think I won't."

"Anyway, I'll be glad to get home," Bethani said. "Not to go back to school, but to see what's been happening while we were away."

"I bet Hope and Faith have grown since I saw them last week!" A melancholy note slipped into Megan's voice. She kept the Montgomery almost-twins whenever she could. Bethani often helped Genny out at *New Beginnings*, making their 'aunt' wonder what she would do without them when they went off to college.

"And don't forget. I have a baseball game

Monday afternoon," Blake said. "Did you wash my uniform before we left?"

"You wore it," his mother reminded him, "I didn't."

"If not, I bet it can stand up on its own with all that stank," his twin predicted. "But did you remember we all three have an Honor Society program this week, to induct new members and incoming officers?"

"And I have an interview to apply for a new program the university is offering this year," Megan added. "I think my mom is taking me, but she may have a photography session planned. Everyone is scheduling senior pictures, and she has some big wedding coming up with Bridezilla herself. If she can't go, can you, Mama Maddy?"

"And," Brash said, drawing out the word.

Something about the way he said it made Madison look at him closely. She knew that tone. What had he kept from her? "Why do I think I'm not going to like whatever it is you're about to say?"

"Because you may not like what I'm about to say. Then again, you may."

She made an impatient wave with her hand. "Just tell me and be done with it."

"We're having company when you get home."

"What? Are you serious? We've been gone for a week. I haven't done any grocery shopping. I'll have a ton of laundry to do, *plus* all the things the kids just mentioned. I can't—"

He broke into her rant. "It's Roberts and Patty. For now, the Big House is their safe house."

This time, her "What?" didn't sound nearly as irritated. "They're staying with us?"

"It seemed to be the best solution until the DA can make long-term arrangements. Tar-Go will have no reason to look for them in The Sisters. And on the off chance they do, we have an excellent security system at the house. You don't mind, do you?"

"No, of course not. It actually makes sense."

"I thought you would say that, or I wouldn't have suggested it. But I couldn't tell you at the inn in case someone should overhear."

"This is so awesome!" Bethani cooed. "We'll get to spend more time with Patty."

"Yes but remember... No one can know they're there. She can't go out with you and risk being seen. Everyone understand?"

"Got it, Dad," Megan said.

"We'd never do anything to cause her more danger," Blake agreed. "She's been through too much already."

"I agree," Madison said. "And I don't have any problem with them being there. But," she added on a sigh, "I still have to go grocery shopping."This time, her "What?" didn't sound nearly as irritated. "They're staying with us?"

"It seemed to be the best solution until the DA can make long term arrangements. Tar-Go will have no reason to look for them in The Sisters. And on the off chance they do, we have an excellent security system at the house. You don't mind, do you?"

"No, of course not. It actually makes sense."

"I thought you would say that, or I won't have

suggested it. But I couldn't tell you at the inn, in case someone should overhear."

"This is so awesome!" Bethani cooed. "We'll get to spend more time with Patty."

"Yes, but remember. No one can know they're there. She can't go out with you and risk being seen. Everyone understand?"

"Got it, Dad," Megan said.

"We'd never do anything to cause her more danger," Blake agreed. "She's been through too much already."

"I agree," Madison said. "And I don't have any problem with them being there. But," she added on a sigh, "I still have to go grocery shopping."

22

Madison knew she had a busy week in store. Not only were there loads of laundry and a to-do list that seemed to never end, but she had to host the Robertses without anyone knowing about it.

That included her own grandmother, who Madison was now visiting. She had told Granny Bert she was already out running errands and would drop by her house, but the truth was Madison was trying to keep her away from the Big House. She wasn't sure how long she could keep up the charade, but she would give it her best try.

Once they were seated at the old kitchen table, Granny Bert gave her an update on their strange new client.

"Is she senile?" Madison asked. "Suffer from dementia?"

"Clinically speaking, neither of those. That's according to her daughter. Personally, I think the old bat's not only missing a few screws, I think the whole toolbox is gone."

"Granny, what a thing to say!"

"You haven't met her. Haven't seen the change that comes over her when she talks about the past, especially her father and someone named Gracie. And she insists that a tree in the backyard is evil. I'm telling you; the toolbox is gone."

"An evil tree? That's a little odd," Madison agreed.

Her grandmother sat back and crossed her arms over her chest. "Just ask me why the tree is evil."

"Why is the tree evil?"

"Because that's where the bodies are buried."

"Bodies?" Her voice hitched up a note.

"That's what she says."

"Are we assuming she means pets? You know, like when we were kids, and the boy cousins would kill birds with their BB guns? Hallie and I would have funeral services for them, burying them in shallow graves and saying a few words and songs over their poor, lost souls, cut short in flight." Madison tried looking hopeful. "Is that what she meant?"

"Would a few buried birds make a tree evil?"

"Maybe not birds," she amended. "Maybe a favorite pet. Maybe she associates the tree with her pet's death. Not that tree, of course, but one like it."

"I think it was that tree. In fact, I think she grew up in that house."

"Did you ask Banisha?"

"Tried. She doesn't like talking about the past any more than her mother does. Ella says her daughter thinks she's above her raising. I suspect it's because she came up poor, and now she's got a fancy career and an uppity husband. She doesn't want to give credit to the woman who raised her and the roots that helped her grow. Her sisters sound even worse."

It was one of her grandmother's pet peeves. Before she climbed on her soap box and preached about family roots and staying true to one's self, Madison went back to the subject of the tree.

"So, it's the tree that causes Ella the most stress."

"Yep. Insists it's evil. Brings up shovels and digging holes and hiding the shovel where no one can find it."

"Why would she hide a shovel?"

"Because of the blood."

"What blood?"

"The blood that was on their clothes, the ones they burned, or something to that order. I'm telling you, the woman either has a wild imagination, or something traumatic has happened in the past."

"What did you say her maiden name was?"

"I didn't, but it was Marsh. None of us remember a Marsh family ever living here."

"If you don't remember," Madison reasoned, "then there's probably no reason to look it up on the internet. Your little network of spies is better than any search engine."

"We aren't spies." Her grandmother took offense. "And we aren't gossip mongers. We're searchers of the truth. Knowledge gatherers. We ferret out little nuggets of useful information that might otherwise be overlooked."

"That's just a fancy way of saying all of you are nosy."

Her smug expression held no remorse. "Comes in handy sometimes, too, doesn't it, girl? And the apple doesn't fall far from the tree. I think it bounced off your father's head and landed smack-dab on you. You're as nosy as me." She looked oddly proud of that fact.

"Maybe," Madison agreed. On a serious note, she asked, "Do you believe in supernatural powers? Like the ability to know what people are thinking and feeling?"

"I raised four boys. It's called survival—mine and theirs—not supernatural."

"I don't mean a mother's spidey sense. I mean like knowing what a person needs before they even know they need it. Like an indiscernible connection that draws people to you. Before they even meet you."

Granny Bert cocked her gray head. "I'm not sure I understand."

Madison pushed out a sigh. "I'm not sure I do, either, but Sirenity does."

"Then maybe we should call her up here to figure out Ella Getty, because I sure can't! When you meet her, you'll know what I mean. Just you wait."

"Why do I have to meet her? You took her on as a client, not me."

"Because we have to put you on the rotation. Like I said, Sybil's not cut out to handle an old bird like Ella Getty."

"She handles you, doesn't she?"

"That's different. Sybil's known me her whole life. Plus, I don't go off on innocent trees. I love trees."

"I still don't see why the other three of you can't pick up the slack."

"To be honest with you, that woman plumb tuckers us all out," her grandmother finally confessed.

Humor hovered around Madison's lips. "You mean to tell me that someone finally got the best of Bertha Hamilton Cessna?"

"Not the best!" Granny Bert snapped. "But it wears a soul out, dealing with that crazy talk of hers and trying to get her back inside the house."

"Then don't take her outside."

"It's not that easy, Miss Smartypants. Sometimes she just goes off. She'll bring up the subject of her old pappy or this Gracie gal. If we say one word—a question about them or sometimes just a nod of understanding—she gets belligerent. Says she never talks about *that*."

"That?"

"What she calls some traumatic event in her past. Or maybe it only happened in her head. She gets a little fuzzy on the details, even when she's just talking to herself. And once Ella thinks about whatever it is that haunts her, she's in a snit the rest of the afternoon. Nothing we do pleases her."

"Sort of like someone else I know when she's in the hospital." Madison gave her grandmother a knowing eye.

"But she's not in a hospital. And she's not in a nursing home, either, because she keeps getting kicked out!"

"I don't know if I can squeeze her into my schedule this week. It's already pretty full."

"We have you down for Tuesday."

"But—"

"Just remember not to take her out to the back porch and not to mention anything about the past. Got it?"

"I got that you've somehow pulled me into another of your schemes," Madison muttered.

"One of the many perks of being my granddaughter." Granny Bert's smile looked serene, as if she actually expected Madison to thank her.

Madison rolled her eyes. She *so* wished she were back at the beach!

As if her grandmother weren't a handful, Madison had to deal with Derron the next day.

He was late getting to work, which had become the norm for him. He was always quick to point out that he was efficient, if not conventional. And it was true. Late arrivals, extended lunch breaks, and afternoons off didn't keep him from getting his work done.

"It's nice to have you join me this morning," Madison said in a droll voice.

"Says the woman who was off for an entire week. How was your relaxing week at the beach?"

"Not very relaxing."

"I'd say I'm sorry, but I had a hellacious week, myself." He went off on a list of so-called travesties that had happened to him while she was gone, none of which were more than a mild hiccup. He concluded with, "Plus, GB added insult to injury by calling an emergency meeting. On a Friday night! Not to mention that *someone* sent me off on a wild goose chase looking for a man named Bob Smith. I spent an entire day looking up millions of Bob Smiths, and you didn't have the decency to tell me you'd already found him!"

"I found him on my own, early the very next morning," she pointed out.

"But you didn't inform *me* of that for another day!"

"Which means you put off doing it. What was more important than doing your assignment?"

"It was already mid-afternoon," he whined. "And my favorite boutique was having a sale. But enough about that. This week isn't starting off much better, either. I waited forever for Wanda to bring me breakfast in bed. Turns out she's down in the back for some reason. Personally, I think it was the game of Twister she played with Ella Getty, but she'd never admit it."

"Wait." Madison put up a hand to stop him, shaking her head in amazement. "There are so many things wrong with that statement, I can't even comprehend them. First of all, you're a grown man, and Wanda is in her eighties. If anything, *you* should be taking breakfast to *her*. And Twister? Really? At her age? And with a woman we're supposed to be taking care of?"

"That's what your grandmother said, but Wanda insists Ella enjoyed it."

"Have you met this Ella?"

"No, and I don't want to! She sounds possessed. They said she even talks in a strange voice when she's reliving a scene from the past, like she's truly filled with an inner spirit. Wanda thinks we should have an exorcism and drive the demons away. What do you think? Is it worth a try?"

"Wh— An exorcism?" Madison asked incredulously. "Has everyone lost their minds?"

"You mean, besides Ella? Because that woman has definitely lost hers."

"I have a headache," Madison mumbled, rubbing her forehead, "and the day's just started. And before you even ask, you cannot have the afternoon off. I'm meeting Genny for a late lunch."

"I wouldn't think of leaving early," Derron assured her. He pranced to his desk and turned to casually ask, "Did I mention I'm taking the day off tomorrow?"

"Oh, no, you're not. Because I won't be here."

"Again? You just got back!" he whined.

"Somehow, I got suckered into watching Ella Getty tomorrow. You'll have the office to yourself, and you'd better be here. The entire day." She stabbed him with a threatening glare.

"Okay, okay. Take it easy. Just because your grandmother swindled you into doing something you don't want to do, don't take it out on me."

She wasn't backing off. "You work here, Derron. Oh, and don't go in the main part of the house." She could set a lockout code to enforce the warning, but she needed a plausible reason. Derron was like family. "We're having it exterminated early in the morning, and the smell may be stout. If you promise not to stay gone long, you can order something from Genny's and put it on my tab."

He was easily persuaded with the bribe. "Deal," he agreed.

Her lunch with Genny was much more relaxing. The best friends caught up with all the happenings of the past week, oohed over Genny's latest pictures of the girls and Madison's pictures of the beach, and made vague plans for a dinner party with Laurel and Cade.

As they lingered over coffee and Gennydoodle cookies, Madison asked, "Do you know Banisha Vickers?"

"Not very well. I've seen her at the bank, and she's an occasional customer. Nothing fried, and nothing too Southern. She prefers my trendier options, like couscous and tilapia in dill sauce."

"Her mother is living with her now, and she hired the Geriatric Crew to sit with her until she finds another nursing home for her."

"I heard something about her mother having trouble staying in a home," Genny nodded. "What seems to be the problem?"

"Acting out and having a very vivid imagination. They say she's too disruptive for the other residents."

"And you let Granny Bert and Wanda Shanks sit with her?" She looked as dubious as Blake had been.

"They took the assignment upon themselves. But even Granny Bert admits she's a handful."

"I've never met her. But it's the only time Banisha's ever ordered meatloaf or old-fashioned pot roast. She says her mother is difficult to please, but she likes comfort food."

"And lucky me gets to sit with her tomorrow. Apparently, she's too much for Miss Sybil, so they put me on the rotation without asking me."

"Miss Sybil is more delicate and soft hearted than the others," Genny agreed. The door chimed, and Genny smiled. "And look! There she comes now." She waved her over.

After hugs and greetings all around, Madison scooted over and invited her to join them at the back booth.

"How was the beach, dear?" she asked.

Glossing over the harsher truths of the week, she answered with a smile. "My time there didn't last long enough."

"Well, we certainly missed you here."

"I hear you ladies took on a new client while I was gone."

"Yes, but that may have been a mistake. You know I don't like to talk bad about people, but she's difficult, to say the least."

"Granny Bert said you're trying to find out about her past. Any luck?"

"Not much," the older woman sighed. "A few folks have a vague recollection of a Marsh family that lived here a long time ago. But something happened, and they moved away."

"What happened?"

"No one will say. Most likely, they don't know, or else it would be on everyone's tongues."

"Hmm. I think I'll check the county records and see if Banisha's house was once the old Marsh place."

"It was. I called my niece who works in the tax office. She says someone has kept up with the taxes all these years, but it lay abandoned until Banisha moved in. Some of the place was sold off, most likely to pay taxes on the house and a few acres around it. Kinda strange that no one ever lived there for over six decades, don't you think?"

"This is a small community," Genny pointed out. "Not much of a workforce here."

"But all that land, and that lovely old house, just going to waste! It's a shame," Miss Sybil tsked.

"Banisha and her husband are there now," Genny reminded her, "so it's not going to waste any longer. Someone's made it into a home again."

"And, for now, anyway," Madison added, "Ella Getty is back in her childhood home."

"She doesn't seem too happy about it, though," Miss Sybil said. "Something about that house haunts her. Not spirits, mind you, but some dark memory. I think she's blocked it from her mind because it's too painful to recall."

"That's possible," Madison agreed. "I just wonder what it was that happened out there."

"That's what I'm trying to find out, dear," Miss Sybil said, patting her arm with a reassuring smile. "I think Thelma has my order ready. I called in something to take over to Wanda. She's not feeling so spry today. Poor dear pulled her back."

"Derron says it was from playing Twister with Ella."

"Don't," Miss Sybil warned emphatically, "get your grandmother started on that subject. She walked in on them and says it wasn't a pretty sight. Especially since she had to crawl in under Wanda and rescue Ella." At the look on the other women's faces, she held up her hand. "Don't ask. None of us want to know the details."

"Not a word," Madison promised. She pretended to zip her lips and throw away the key. She tried her best not to visualize the picture Miss Sybil had painted with the story, but she could already see it in her head.

Granny Bert was right. It wasn't a pretty picture.

23

Madison showed up with a big smile and a positive attitude the next morning, determined to make the best of her day with Ella Getty.

"I know you from somewhere," the old woman grunted. She squinted her eyes to look at her better. "Did you ever work at The Rosewood?"

"No, ma'am."

"The Billington House?"

"Not there, either."

Ella's mouth curled in distaste. "The Safe Haven?" She practically spat the name.

"No, ma'am. I've never worked in any of those places."

"But I've seen you somewhere…" she insisted.

Madison shrugged. "I guess I just have one of those faces."

"I've got it! I've seen you on TV! You were on a game show."

"Not a game show." She neither denied nor confirmed the television part.

"Hold it. Now I've got it! It was one of those

reality shows, but it was about a house. Juliet Blakesly's old house, I do believe. The Big House."

Madison hesitantly admitted, "Yes, that's right. I live in the Big House now."

"Juliet Blakesly was a snooty old gal," Ella said.

Her words took Madison by surprise. "You knew her?" This definitely confirmed she had lived here before.

"Everyone in these parts knew her. Or about her. And her sister, too. Those two were always squabbling."

"That's what I hear. I used to go with Granny Bert to visit her. I always loved that house."

Ella turned up her nose. "If you like gaudy old mansions, I guess it will do."

Sensing a shift in moods, Madison said, "So, you watched the show?"

"Not me. But Ralph enjoyed it."

"And Ralph was…?"

"The reason I got kicked out of Renewed Hope! We were just having a little fun. What's the harm in taking a walk in the garden? Or a shower at two o'clock in the morning? They had too many rules. They made me wear that bracelet."

"A bracelet?"

"Aren't you keeping up with the conversation?" she barked. "They made me wear a bracelet, so they could track me whenever I sneaked off to be with Ralph. They didn't understand that we were free spirits, and that we just needed a little spice in our lives. They dang sure didn't put any on their food," she grumbled. "Worse slop you ever did taste. Worse than Banisha's fancy cooking, and that's saying something."

"I understand you like the food at *New Beginnings,* though."

"Is that where my daughters are sending me to next? This *New Beginnings* place?"

"It's a restaurant in town. My best friend owns it."

"I think I remember that from the show. The cute blonde and the sexy firefighter."

Madison nodded with a smile. "That would be Genny and Cutter."

Ella sniffed. "They were the most interesting thing about the show. Them, and that fine-looking policeman. What was his name? Ralph would get jealous, because the men were the only reason I watched the show with him."

"Brash. Brash deCordova."

"You were a nitwit for not knowing a good thing when you saw it," Ella said bluntly. "I would have been all over that man like white on rice!"

Madison cringed and remained silent.

"What happened in the end? I think that was about the time they made me move."

"The house turned out beautiful, and I ended up marrying the handsome police officer."

"At least you finally came to your senses!" Ella huffed.

"Better late than never. Would you like more coffee?"

"No, not without some of Gracie's cookies. I don't suppose we have any of those left?"

"I'm afraid not."

"I guess *he* ate them all." Her eyes turned dark and troubled.

Wow. It's taken me less than thirty minutes to set her off. Way to go, Maddy, she chastised herself.

"Maybe you'd like to watch some television? Granny Bert said you liked to watch the morning game shows."

"Too early."

"We could do a puzzle," Madison suggested. "I hear you like to put together jigsaw puzzles. So do I."

"I started a new one this weekend."

"Good. Let's go work on it. Do you need help?"

"Walking? No! I learned how to do that almost eighty years ago. Now get out of my way, and I'll show you."

They had worked on the puzzle for a half hour or more. Ella enjoyed it, and even laughed a few times at something Madison said. She was feeling hopeful when it all came screeching to a halt.

"Is that... Is that a *tree?*" Ella demanded, pointing at a section Madison had just completed.

Wishing she could rearrange the puzzle pieces and turn them into something else, Madison could only weakly admit, "Yes, ma'am."

"How dare you? How dare you bring up a tree in this house! I told you we are *never* to speak of that day again!" With a sweep of her arm, Ella pushed the half-finished puzzle off the table. The box tumbled with it, sending a thousand pieces onto the floor.

"I'm sorry. I didn't realize..."

"You have to think for yourself, Gracie! I can't

always do it for both of us. You can't be so careless. Now look at the mess you've made."

Maybe I caught her on a bad day, Madison decided.

"And that tree is evil!" Ella snapped. "Promise me you won't go near it. Promise, Gracie." She reached out to grasp her companion's arm.

"I—I promise," Madison replied. Ella's grip was far stronger than she would have expected.

"We did what we had to do. We did it for you. And we won't talk about it again, is that clear?"

Madison nodded, even though nothing was clear.

"I know you're simple minded, Gracie. That's why it's easy for people to take advantage of you. That's why Pappy and I have to look out for you. So that no one else can hurt you. Do you understand what I'm saying?"

Madison nodded a second time.

"Get out of those torn clothes and clean yourself up. I'll burn our clothes, so no one will see the blood. Then get back down here and fix supper. Pappy will be mighty hungry after all this."

Madison had no idea what was going on, but it sent an eerie chill down her back. In spite of Ella's intense words, her voice had a gentle quality to it, as if she were speaking to a child. Madison had to wonder how old this Gracie person was.

She sat still, waiting to take her cue from Ella. With her next breath, would she be this compassionate person from the past, or the current cranky version of herself?

She seemed to be a mix of the two.

"You can clean this later," Ella said amicably. "Let's watch my game shows."

The softer, likable Ella Getty lasted until after lunch when she insisted on going outside.

"We can't. It looks like rain," Madison fibbed.

"There's a porch. We won't get wet."

"The weatherman called for a blowing rain. I think it's best if we stay in."

"Well, I don't. I want to go outside," she said stubbornly.

"Again, it's supposed to rain." Madison reminded her.

"Then I *especially* want to go outside. Maybe it will come a true gully-washer. Enough to wash away the roots on that evil tree out there! I want to see that. I want to see that tree wash away and be gone, once and for all."

Madison had nothing to lose. Ella was already working herself into a snit.

"But what about what's buried beneath the tree?" Madison asked softly. "What if it washes that up, too?"

Ella's face lost some of its color. "You—You know about that? How? Who told you?"

Madison took a gamble. "I saw you with the shovel."

"I—I only did what Pappy told me to do. We didn't know what else to do. And there was all that blood. It was everywhere."

"So, you burned the clothes."

"Yes! Yes, that's exactly what we did. And we

never mentioned it again. Not to anyone."

"Maybe it's time you talked about it, Ella," Madison said softly. "Maybe it's time you got this off your chest. I can see it's been bothering you all these years."

"Of course it has! But I promised Pappy. He told me to hide the shovel, and I did. He told me to never talk about it again, and I haven't. I can't start now." She looked at Madison with defiance in her eyes. "And you can't make me!"

Madison knew she had missed her window of opportunity. Just for a moment, when she caught Ella with her guard down, she thought she could coax her into talking. But the moment was lost, swept away by another of the woman's mood swings.

"You're right, Ella. I can't make you talk to me. But if you ever want to, I'm here to listen."

"I won't," she assured her coldly.

"Hey. I saw a cute cat puzzle there on the shelf. Would you like to put it together?"

"Cats?"

"Yes. Dozens of little furry, playful kittens."

"I like kittens." The old woman smiled.

"Good. Let's go do a puzzle."

Madison gave herself a pat on the back. She had managed to divert a major meltdown.

Madison stopped by the police station on the way home.

Brash greeted her with a surprised smile. "To what do I owe this honor, Mrs. deCordova? Miss me that much? I'll be home in an hour or so."

"Yes, I did miss you, but that's not the only reason I stopped by."

"I didn't think so. What's the real reason?"

"Can you look up a cold case for me?"

"How cold?"

"Sixty years cold."

"So, ice cold," he translated. "Sort of like the other cold cases you've asked me to look into. Again, I'm not sure how good of records they kept back then, but I'll see what I can find. But there's an easier way, you know. Just ask your grandmother."

"That's the weird thing. Even she doesn't know. Nobody does."

"What case is it? Who am I looking up?"

"That's the tricky part," she confessed. "I don't exactly know. All I have is a last name. Marsh."

"Why does this remind me of the search for Bob Smith?" he mumbled under his breath.

"It has something to do with Ella Getty, the new client Granny Bert accepted without talking to me about. Her maiden name was Marsh, and they lived here when she was young. I don't know her parents' names, but they had a farm out of Naomi. Banisha and Al Vickers renovated the old homestead and live there now."

"Farmers in the aftermath of the Great Depression. Hmm, that really narrows things down," he said with heavy sarcasm.

"It involves someone named Gracie. I think she was Ella's younger sister. And something bad happened, but I have no idea what. Something no one wants to talk about. Are you writing this down?"

"Don't need to. Have it all up here," he said, tapping his temple.

Madison looked doubtful. "Maybe I'll ask your mom. She knows almost as much local history as Granny Bert does."

"She does, but she's bogged down with this deCordova genealogy project of hers. She's trying to talk my father into going to Spain next year. She wants to track down some conquistador named deCordova. I lost track at how many great-great-greats are involved, but somewhere down the line, he's my grandfather."

"That sounds interesting. Hey, why don't we make it a foursome and go along with them? I'd love to know more about your family history, and I've always wanted to go to Spain!"

"Maddy," he said, giving her a stern but loving look. It matched the timbre of his voice. "You've already planned a half-dozen trips for us. I know what you're doing. You think if we stay busy enough, we won't miss the kids as much when they go to college."

She looked down at her hands. "But that big old house will be so empty without them. I know Megan only lives with us part of the time, but I just can't imagine that house without all three of them in it."

"Sweetheart, all three of them are going to colleges here in Texas. It's not like they'll only come home on holidays."

"But I know how it is. They'll get involved with new friends and new organizations, and they may even get jobs while there. They won't have time to come home."

"They'll be back, Maddy. They'll be home over the summers, so it's not like they're moving away forever."

"But I met Gray in college, and I moved away forever."

"Until you moved back here," he pointed out.

"Twenty years later! I don't want my children to be gone for the next twenty years!"

"Sweetheart," he said, coming around his desk to gather her in his arms. "We're not losing our kids. We're giving them—"

"Do not say wings. Don't you dare say wings."

"Fine. We're giving them a chance to be normal, healthy young adults. It's part of the growing-up process. It's our job as parents."

"Can't you just agree with me and stop being so right all the time?"

"Later, when you aren't so upset, I'll point out that you just admitted I'm always right."

"Don't count on it," she said, but she did crack a small smile. "But seriously. This isn't a laughing matter, Brash. And neither is whatever happened out at the Marsh homestead. Just see what you dig up, okay?" She winced when she realized her poor choice of words.

"Don't get your hopes up. I may have to chip off a few hunks of ice just to find something."

"Just try." She brushed a kiss across his lips. "I'll go home and start supper. We have guests, after all."

"Which you're being a very good sport about."

"I don't mind at all. I know it's not easy on them, either."

Brash trusted everyone in The Sisters Police Department without question, but he still lowered his voice to ask, "Derron hasn't suspected anything?"

She shook her head. "I bribed him with a free lunch today, but I don't know what excuse I'll use tomorrow."

"Or if you need one," Brash said.

"But we usually find a bite to eat in the kitchen," she pointed out.

"Maybe," he said, a merry twinkle in his brown eyes, "you'll luck out, and Nancy Nguyen will bring fried rice and eggrolls."

"I keep telling her she's more than paid me for helping her son, but she still insists on feeding us occasionally," Madison marveled. "That woman is amazing."

"And so is the one I married," he said. He showed his appreciation with a kiss, before releasing her and telling her goodbye.

24

"How was your day in the loony bin?" Derron asked the next morning, his mood surprisingly chipper. He was even on time.

"A little strange. Okay, a lot strange," Madison admitted. "But I did get glimpses of a sane, perfectly normal woman. She even has a sense of humor."

"When she's not possessed, you mean."

"She's not possessed. Not by demons, anyway. Just by her memories. Something dark happened to her, and she's never gotten over it."

"We all have our demons to bear. Mine was the Dragon Lady."

"Darla was your mother, Derron."

"She gave birth to me, yes. But we never had a fuzzy, parent-child relationship. And while we're on the subject of demons and dragons, my aunt called today."

Madison rolled her eyes. "What did Myrna need now?"

"Besides a personality transplant? She wanted to know where you put a particular insurance file."

"How would I know? They haven't hired *In a Pinch* to temp there in well over two years!"

"That's what I said. But according to her, she has meticulous organizational skills, so therefore it has to be your fault."

"I will not dignify that by calling her back."

"She'll still blame you."

"Of course she will. It's Myrna."

"Speaking of Fashion House…"

"We weren't speaking of Fashion House."

"We weren't? But now that you've brought it up—"

"No."

"No, what? I haven't asked a question yet."

"But you will. You'll tell me about some fabulous sweater you found, and that it goes off sale tomorrow."

"Tonight at eight."

"Which you'll have plenty of time to make when you get off work. At the regular time and not before."

"Who are you this week? Vacation just made you mean, not relaxed."

"I'm your boss, Derron. And we actually have work to do, so let's do it."

"Fine, fine. I was going to surprise you by buying you a sweater, too, but never mind. If you want to continue to dress like your grandmother, far be it from me to spruce up your wardrobe."

"It's getting too warm for sweaters."

"Cashmere is always in season, dollface."

"So is work."

"But there's nothing to do. We're all caught up. We don't have any other jobs lined up until next week."

"Then you can help me with this job."

"I told you; I don't do creepy. And Ella Getty sounds creepy. Just wait until her head turns around backwards on her neck."

"I just need you to look up some nursing homes for me on the computer. She mentioned some yesterday, and I wonder what was so bad about them."

"I thought she was the one who was bad, not them."

"But there was one in particular that sounded worse than the others. When she said its name, she looked like she had eaten a lemon."

"What was it?"

"I don't remember which one it was," Madison admitted. "Try the Billington House."

He confirmed the towns and areas he needed to search. After a few taps on his computer, Derron asked, "The Billington House at Parker's Point? What's so bad about this? It looks lovely."

"Okay, try something about Roses."

"Would that be roses spelled with Bob Smith, or with a R?"

"Very funny. Try... The Rosewood. I think that was one of them."

Again, he reported, "Looks fine to me. All five-star ratings. Testimonials a mile long. Residents and their families all love it."

"What about New Hope? No, wait. Renewed Hope."

It took only a few minutes to report much the same thing. "Looks fine. There was an on-going battle by one family to have a relative reinstated, but they lost the case and filed a complaint. This could have been your friend, because that's the only negative thing I see about it, other than the food. A lot of people weren't impressed by it."

"That's what Ella said. Okay, there was one more. It had an odd name for a nursing home." She tapped her fingers on her chin. "Oh, I remember. Safe Haven."

It took a few moments before he grunted and gave a low whistle. "What do you know."

"What? What did you find?"

"It's an odd name for a nursing home because it's not a nursing home. It's a wacko ward for the mentally insane."

"A mental institute?"

"See, I told you. Ella Getty is certifiable."

"I'm not so sure about that. And you can't call it a wacko ward. Those people have legitimate issues, either mental or emotional."

"Well, Ella was obviously a patient here, so that proves she has issues. I still say she's—oh, wait. You may be right. It says that Safe Haven was only open for less than a year. It burned to the ground in 1947. All of the residents inside perished."

"That's horrible!"

"Not exactly a safe haven, huh?"

Something tugged at Madison's memory.

When Ella thought she was speaking to Gracie, she had called the girl simple minded.

"Derron, do you think you could get a list of patients' names who died in that fire?"

"I don't know. What with all the privacy laws and such—"

"Which weren't in effect back then. See what you can find, please. I have a hunch."

Shortly before lunch, Granny Bert called.

"We have a problem."

"What's that?"

"Virgie is at Ella's, but Hank had some sort of spell, and she needs to take him to the doctor."

"Is he okay?"

"He sounds pretty shook up. The thing is, she'll have to leave Ella there alone."

"And?" She knew there had to be an *and* or *but* in there somewhere for her grandmother to have called.

"Wanda's back is still giving her fits, so I brought her over to her doctor. So that leaves you."

"Me?"

"That, or we pull Banisha from her job, which means she'll pull us from ours."

"I get it, Granny. You don't want her to fire us." She huffed out a sigh. "Okay, I'll go."

"Right now."

"I'm grabbing my purse as we speak."

Derron looked up in concern. "Where do you think you're going?"

"Emergency. I have to take over at Ella Getty's." Remembering she didn't have an excuse to keep him from the main part of the house, she said, "You know what? Go ahead and leave. I wouldn't want you to miss your sale."

She was out the door before he could shower her with accolades about being the best boss ever.

She was no more out of her car at the Vickers' when Virgie met her outside. "She's taking a nap," the elderly woman said hurriedly, "so things are peaceful now. I have to go."

"I hope Mr. Hank is okay," Madison called to her receding back.

She knew Ella would be confused when she awoke and found someone else was her caregiver, but the woman seemed to take it in stride.

"Hello, Miss Ella," Madison said when the woman roused. "Surprise. I'm back."

"I can see that. Where's the other one?"

"Miss Virgie? She had an emergency and had to leave."

"Okay. What's for lunch?"

Madison hoped it was a sign that today would be easier than the day before.

Lunch went well, and then Ella wanted to work on her jigsaw puzzle.

"It's starting to take shape," Madison said with a smile. "I see at least two kittens."

"These don't make you sneeze?"

"Sneeze? Why would they?"

"You always sneeze when you're around cats. Pappy said that's why we have to keep ours in the barn."

Madison realized she thought she was talking

to Gracie again. "It's okay. These don't bother me."

After a moment, Ella said, "That's how I know you've been to the barn. You came back in sneezing."

"Oh."

"Pappy warned you about him, Gracie. He's nothing but a no-good drifter. You steer clear of that man. Especially in the barn and the cornfield."

"Okay."

"I mean it, girl. His kind are bad news. I've seen the way he looks at you. You stay away from him, you hear me?"

"Okay, Ella. I will," Madison said, hoping she said the right thing.

"Good. Just remember that, and it will be okay. Why don't you stir up a batch of your special cookies? They always make things better."

It seemed to Madison that Gracie did all the cooking. Had they taken advantage of the girl because she had a simple mind?

"Do you know how to cook, Ella?" she asked.

"Of course, I know how to cook. Mama taught me, same as she taught you."

Madison pushed her luck. "But I do all the cooking."

"That's just the way it is, Gracie. It's all you know. Pappy can't read or write, so I do all the ciphering and ordering and paying for goods. I work the fields with him. I work as hard as any man. The least you can do is keep up with the household chores."

Madison didn't know how to respond to that, so she said nothing.

"I'm tired," Ella announced suddenly. "I want to take a nap."

She settled in her recliner and was soon snoring. Madison used the opportunity to open emails on her phone and respond to those most urgent.

It startled her when Ella cried out in her sleep. "No!" She twisted in her chair, moving her head back and forth. "No, stop it!" She moaned, most of her words too mumbled and low to understand. Only a few came out clearly enough to distinguish.

Hurt... Get away... Not Gracie.

Madison wondered what the words meant. What had happened here? Why did it still haunt the old woman? Whatever it was, it had tortured her for decades.

Maybe, Madison decided, if she could help her find closure, she could finally be at peace.

"Ella," she said softly. "I didn't hear you. What did you say?"

She said the same words, but this time, she mentioned shovels. And blood.

And bodies.

Madison was too spooked to ask anything else.

She called her grandmother on the way home. "Are you still at the doctor's office?"

"No, we're home now. He gave Wanda some muscle relaxers and told her to take it easy for a few days."

"What about Mr. Hank? Have you heard

anything?"

"It turns out his sodium was out of whack. Made him plumb crazy, slurring his words and stumbling all over the place. They're keeping him overnight, but he should be able to come home tomorrow."

"That's good. So, you're on duty with Ella tomorrow?"

"Sounds like it. How was she today?"

"Not as belligerent, but clearly confused. She keeps thinking I'm Gracie."

"Did you learn anything else? Has she said anything?"

"Nothing that makes sense. But I did want to ask you something. Didn't you tell me something about hobos and them knowing which houses to stop at?"

"Yes. Some walked, but a lot traveled by rail car, sneaking aboard until they were either kicked off or came to the next town. They looked for houses that had a symbol outside that let them know they were welcome. Some folks offered them a hot meal or a cool drink of water. Others offered their barn for the night."

"Were those the same as drifters?"

"Not always. Hobos were mostly harmless, just down on their luck. But drifters were often up to no good. Usually looking for a way to take advantage of people before moving on to the next person."

"Sounds like the same thing to me."

"Hobos usually offered to do odds jobs to pay for their keep. Most didn't want handouts, just a place to rest. Drifters might sound helpful at first and offer to do something nice, like muck out a barn or repair a fence, but then they expected money. Sometimes, they were working a scheme, trying to pull a fast one on unsuspecting folks. They tended to overstay their welcome, until they met up with the wrong end of a shotgun."

"They sound worse than telemarketers," Madison grumbled.

"Why all the questions?"

"Ella said something about a drifter. Said he was up to no good."

"That sounds about right."

"She warned Gracie about going near him. And I think Gracie was her sister. She was what Ella called simple minded, so Gracie did all the cooking and cleaning, and Ella did everything else. Which, apparently, included all the thinking for her sister. And the reading and writing for her father."

"Back then, a lot of folks didn't bother with learning to read. Especially farmers. They knew the things they needed to know. They got by well enough to provide for their families."

"What usually happened to girls like Gracie? The simple-minded ones?"

"They usually found a husband. Someone looking for a cook and a warm body in bed, more than intellectual conversation. If they didn't marry and were lucky, they found work, usually as a cook for some rich family. But a lot of them never left home. They depended on their family to take care of them for their whole lives."

"I don't think that was the case here. I think something happened to Gracie. I think that's what haunts Ella."

"Like what?"

"I don't know yet. But I intend to find out. Oh, I have to go. This is Derron." She switched over to the waiting call. "Derron?"

"Just letting you know I worked my magic and found that list of names for you before I left. I put it on your desk. And in case you were worried about it, I made it to my sale in plenty of time to buy that lovely yellow sweater."

She was hardly worried, but she murmured, "That's good. And thanks for doing the report before you left. I'll look at it as soon as I get home."

"Talk to you later, dollface. Tootles."

She called Brash next. "I know it's probably too soon, but did you find anything about a cold case back in the day?"

"I looked, but there was nothing to find without more concrete information."

"It may have included a drifter."

"Then I doubt it would have been in a police report."

"Why do say that?"

"They were drifters. No name, no permanent address. They were always on the move. No one really kept up with them."

"What if they committed a crime?"

"Hard to press charges against a moving target."

"What if someone committed a crime against

them?"

"Still wouldn't have made it into a report. Men like that don't want to call attention to themselves. They usually had something to hide, so they wouldn't have filed a report."

"It was just a thought, anyway. I'm probably grasping at straws. Thanks for looking."

"Sorry I couldn't be more help."

"You tried."

"Maddy, if you want answers, have you thought of coming out and just asking her?"

"I have, but she's hard enough to handle now! I don't want a full-blown breakdown on our hands."

"But maybe if she got it out, she could let it go."

"A different version of your river therapy concept?" she teased. Those therapy sessions had always worked on her. Too bad she couldn't take Ella down to the Brazos riverbanks and give his special therapy a try.

"Maybe it's time for another session of our own," Brash suggested. "You've been awfully stressed lately. It may be just the thing you need."

"Maybe," she agreed. "But not until we're done with the Ella Getty mystery, and our guests are gone."

"Banisha hired *In a Pinch* to sit with her mother," he reminded her. "When did it become a mystery?"

Madison sighed. "When Ella told us a tree in her backyard was evil."

25

In 1947, Grace Adaline Marsh was committed to the Renewed Hope Institute for the Mentally Insane. The new facility specialized in treating, caring for, and rehabilitating mentally unstable patients who had a history of violence and abuse. The facility offered the latest in electroshock and artificial fever therapy.

Ten months after the establishment opened its door, a devastating late-night fire swept through the building. All of the residents and in-house personnel perished in the blaze. The only solace for the families was the assumption that most died in their sleep from smoke inhalation.

No wonder Ella was so distraught! It explained so much and yet still left unanswered questions.

Madison had two theories of what had really happened, and she was determined to find out which was correct.

One theory was that after Gracie's tragic death, she and her pappy had held a private burial for the girl, burning her possessions and burying the ashes and her memory under the old oak tree. Being reminded of her death was too painful, so they vowed to never speak of it again.

That theory didn't explain the blood,

however. There was the very real chance the blood was imagined. But if it weren't, Madison had a second theory. Gracie had taken Ella's warnings about the drifter to heart, and the next time he made an advance toward her, Gracie had used a shovel to hurt, or possibly kill, the man. Ella and her pappy had destroyed the evidence, but someone must have known. As punishment, a judge had sentenced her to Renewed Hope for treatment and rehabilitation.

Madison could look up the trial and sentencing records at the county courthouse, but there might be an easier way. If she could get Ella to talk, it would save her the effort.

With that in mind, Madison told her grandmother she would drop in for a visit and bring lunch from *New Beginnings*.

As they ate meatloaf with all the trimmings—mashed potatoes, green beans, and cornbread—Ella seemed to be in a good mood.

"Gracie," she said, "you did a fine job on this meatloaf. Just like our mammy used to make."

Madison sent an *I-told-you-so look* to her grandmother. For whatever reason, Madison reminded Ella of her sister. Since Gracie was presumably simple minded, Madison wasn't sure if it were an insult or a compliment, but today, it gave her the perfect opening she needed.

"Thank you, sister."

Ella looked at her sharply. "Sister?"

"That's what you are, right? My older sister?"

Ella harrumphed. "Goes to show what little you know. I'm your *younger* sister. Not by much, but a year is a year."

"Sorry. You know I'm not good with numbers," Madison mumbled, trying to sound meek.

"That's why I do the thinking for both of us. That's why you must listen to me. We can't talk about that day, Gracie. Not ever!"

"But... the tree..."

A look came over Ella's face, best described as rage. "Is evil! That tree is evil, Gracie! Don't you ever go near it again!"

"Why is it so evil, Ella? It's just a tree."

"A tree with secrets. Deep, dark secrets, deep as its roots. Secrets we can't talk about. So, hush up! I don't want to hear another word about it."

Madison would have pushed for more, but Granny Bert shook her head. *Later,* she mouthed.

They cleaned up the dishes while Ella lingered over dessert. To be so thin, the woman had a healthy appetite.

"Let's work on more of our puzzle, Ella," Madison suggested when the kitchen was clean. "Granny Bert, have you seen the puzzle we're working on? It has kittens on it. Ella likes kittens, don't you, Ella?"

"Yes, but Pappy said we had to keep them in the barn."

Madison and Ella settled at the puzzle table, while Granny Bert sat on the sofa and pulled out her knitting.

"See?" Madison smiled as they worked on the puzzle. "I'm not sneezing. These cats don't bother me."

Ella looked at her strangely. She studied Madison's face with care, as if trying to determine exactly who sat beside her. Madison saw the change in Ella's eyes as her two realities collided. The past and the present.

Madison held her breath, wondering which would prevail.

"That's good, Gracie," Ella finally said.

"I like cats," Madison spoke with care, "but they make me sneeze. That's why I went to the barn. To play with the kittens."

"I told you to keep away from there! That's where *he* stays. You got no business in there, Gracie. Stay in the kitchen where you belong."

Madison sensed this was a common theme in the Marsh household. Gracie was told her only place in the family was more or less as a domestic servant. She was never encouraged to think for herself or to try other skills. Ella didn't have time to cook or clean, so she relegated the duties to her sister.

"Why do you always tell me what to do?" she wondered aloud.

"Because you can't think for yourself! You know that."

Madison imagined what it must have been like for the mentally challenged young woman, always being bossed around, and demeaned by her overbearing sister. She imagined she might have occasionally lashed out with defiance.

"But I like cats," Madison said as Gracie, "and I like the barn, and I like trees. And you can't keep me from them!"

"It's for your own good, and you know it. Don't you remember, Gracie? Don't you remember what happened out there?" Ella's cry sounded distressed.

"No. Tell me what happened."

Stubbornness set in on Ella's face. "I can't. I can't talk about it. We never talk about it."

Madison tossed her head, imagining Gracie might have done the same thing.

"Then I'm getting the kitten, and I'm going to sit under the tree."

Ella moved so quickly Madison didn't have time to react. She grabbed her arm and squeezed tightly.

"Stay. Away. From. That. Barn," she demanded. "And that tree!"

"You—You're hurting me!" Madison said, speaking solely as herself. Ella's fingers dug into her skin.

"*He* hurt you, you stupid girl! Don't you remember anything? Or is your mind too dull?"

Granny Bert stood from the couch, ready to intervene if need be. Ella's aggressive behavior was cause for concern.

"Let go of my arm, Ella."

"Promise me you won't go out there."

"Tell me why I can't," she countered.

Ella released her arm. Oddly enough, she dropped her face into her hands and sobbed. "Was it all for naught? What we did. What we did to protect you. Do you not understand? Was it all for naught? You can't go to that tree! You can't."

Madison looked on helplessly, but she knew

she was close to learning the truth. Brash's words echoed in her head.

...maybe if she got it out, she could let it go...

"I—I think I remember," she told Ella. "He hurt me. He hurt me bad."

"Yes!" Ella looked up, clearly relieved her 'sister' had finally remembered. "I heard a cry, and I thought one of the kittens was hurt. I went to the barn, and he—he was hurting you. Your clothes were torn. Your face was bloody. You—you were screaming for him to stop. But he didn't. He just kept... So, I grabbed the shovel, and I..." Ella was too distraught to go on. Memories washed over her, turning her face pale.

Madison tried not to gasp. She had been wrong about the details. "*You* killed him? I thought Gracie did."

"I had to stop him. He was hurting you."

"What—What happened next? I don't remember."

"Pappy heard the commotion. He saw the shovel. He saw the blood. He—He saw you crying and shivering in the hay. He told me to dig a hole."

It became clear to Madison then. "You buried him under the tree," Madison said in quiet understanding.

"We did what we had to do."

"And you never spoke of it again."

"Did you learn your lesson, Gracie? Do you understand why I know best, and why you must do what I say?"

Madison offered a vague nod. Should she call

Brash? A murder had been committed, but it had been justified.

Hadn't it? It wasn't exactly in self-defense, but she had been protecting her sister. She had acted on impulse.

"I want to lie down now," Ella announced. "In my bed."

Madison and Granny Bert helped her to her room before the two of them collapsed on the couch, emotionally spent.

"Wow," Madison said. "That was unexpected. I thought Gracie had done it."

"How did you know? How did you know it was the drifter?"

"I found out Gracie was committed to a mental facility. She and all the other residents were killed when the building caught fire one night. I knew that had to be part of Ella's grief, but she also talked about a drifter. I mistakenly thought Gracie had killed him and been committed to the facility instead of going to prison."

"What a terrible way to die." Granny Bert shivered.

"I think they never talked about that, either, and I think it all built up until it made Ella sort of crazy, too."

"I didn't get a chance to tell you, but Banisha told me something before she left for work. She said her mother acted very odd last night. Went to bed early, but then they found her taking a shower at two o'clock in the morning. Her feet and the bottom of her gown were dirty, like she had gone outside. She warned me Ella might be in a foul mood today."

"With good reason," Madison sympathized. "Can you imagine what she's had to endure all these years, keeping a secret like that?"

"I guess that's why she thinks the tree is evil. Evil deed, evil secrets."

"I guess." They both sat silently with their thoughts, still reconciling the facts in their minds.

Granny Bert broke the silence. "Do we call Brash?"

"I guess. But I think I need a big glass of water first."

"I'll get it," her grandmother offered. "I need to move around. All this makes me antsy. I'll call Banisha, too. She needs to be here with her mother."

Madison lay her head back against the couch, her mind still going in circles. When she heard Ella up and shuffling toward the living room, she worried she might have fallen asleep and lost track of time.

A quick glance at her watch said that wasn't true. She turned to smile at Ella. "That was certainly a short—"

Madison got no further because Ella saw her there and interrupted.

"What are you doing up, Gracie?" the older woman cried in concern. "You need to be in bed!"

"I'm fine, Ella. It's you who needs to rest."

"Don't go sassing me, girl. You get yourself back to bed. I'll—" she hesitated, her voice oddly shaking, "take care of things."

Madison was shocked to see that Ella carried a shovel. It wasn't old and rusted like the murder weapon must surely be by now, but it was sharp and pointed.

"Ella! Wh—What are you doing? Why do you have that shovel?"

"I'm trying to protect you, girl. You go back to bed before you bleed to death. I'll do it."

"I don't understand." Madison frowned. "Why would I bleed to death?"

"Don't you remember? You just had a baby! He planted his evil seed inside you, girl. Now go back to bed and put that cold press back between your legs. I have to bury the body."

It was another revelation Madison hadn't seen coming. *Gracie had gotten pregnant? The man had attacked her and left her with child?* Her heart went out to the unknown girl, especially knowing the baby had died at birth.

Back in that day, having a child out of wedlock was scandalous. It ruined a woman's reputation, even if she had been raped. It was bad enough that poor Gracie was mentally challenged. Now she was soiled, and no one would ever marry her. Or hire her, for that matter. Her fate was sealed with one terrible act she had had no control over.

Granny Bert came into the living room, carrying two glasses of water. She stopped when she saw the shovel. "What is happening here? Ella, you put that shovel down before someone gets hurt!" she barked.

"I have work to do. I have to hide what she did."

Madison forgot she was playing the part of the

sister. "Surely, you can't blame poor Gracie for getting pregnant."

"Not that. It's what she did after." Ella's chin quivered.

Now Madison was totally confused. "After?"

Ella nodded. She suddenly looked exhausted. The shovel dropped from her hand, and she sank to the couch, almost missing the cushion. Her voice came out hollow as she confessed the worst of her secrets.

"I delivered the baby at home. I only left for a minute, to clean up the mess. But when I came back in, I saw what she had done. I saw the madness in her eyes. No one ever knew. Not even Pappy knew the truth. He believed me when I told him the child was stillborn. We buried the baby under the tree, and we moved away. And we sent Gracie to that home." She crumpled then, sobbing into her hands. "Fire... Lost... Gone forever..."

Granny Bert sat on the couch beside her and took her hand. "We understand, Ella. You did what you had to do. You protected your sister. You kept her secret."

The tortured woman managed to nod. "Never talk about it," she whispered. "Never."

Banisha burst through the door, her eyes expressing equal parts worry and confusion. Madison murmured, "We'll explain later. Your mother needs you right now."

She nodded. "I called my sisters. Told them no excuses, no delays. Just get here." It was heartwarming to see the way she gathered her mother in her arms and comforted her. For someone who had 'gotten above her raising,' she was here now. She didn't know what the problem was, simply that her mother needed her.

In time, after Ella was back in bed and resting peacefully, they told Banisha the full story.

"Thank you," Banisha said. Her dark eyes glistened with tears. "I knew something terrible had happened in her past, but she wouldn't talk about it. What a horrible burden to bear all these years! It explains so much."

"I'm sorry, but I had to call my husband," Madison told her. "He should be here any minute."

After Brash heard the solemn story, he told Banisha, "It happened sixty years ago. All the parties involved are long gone, other than your mother. I do have to report it, but I can't see any prosecutor wanting to press charges. However," he said, his voice compassionate but firm, "it's clear that your mother needs help. I also have to report that. In her state of mind, she could be of danger to herself or someone else."

Banisha nodded. "I understand. And no matter what happens, my sisters and I will be here for her."

26

"What a day!" Madison moaned, too tired to leave the comfort of her SUV's leather seats. Her heart went out to Ella and her entire family for the anguish they had all suffered, directly or indirectly, from one man's horrible actions. She could only hope that Ella found the help she needed. No one should leave this earth with so much sorrow and regret.

Madison closed her eyes for a few moments, collecting her thoughts and her energy. Even though she was more than happy to help the Roberts family and provide them with a safe harbor until permanent arrangements were made, keeping a secret like this from her grandmother and her employee was taking a toll on her nerves.

Granny Bert often stopped back for an impromptu visit, and Madison was afraid she would inadvertently walk in on their guests. The only saving grace was that her grandmother had been preoccupied with Ella Getty this week. But, what about now? With their assignment over—the three sisters were working out a schedule to stay with their mother in lieu of hired sitters—she would have more time on her hands and would likely come by for a visit.

Keeping Derron out of the rest of the house had been a predicament within itself. The *In a Pinch* office was in the stately old mansion's former library, so there was no real distinction between her office and their home. Only a door stood between them. Madison had made several excuses to keep him from going to the kitchen, but it was growing more difficult by the day.

And then, there was the matter of cooking for two extra people. It wasn't a huge inconvenience, but with their erratic schedules and the kids' many different extracurricular activities, it was a complication she didn't have time for.

Idly wondering what she could make with the chicken she had left thawing in the sink, Madison collected her carry-all bag and forced herself out of the car.

On the far side of the sprawling mansion, Derron locked the office door and started for the foot gate. The parking spaces for *In a Pinch* were open to the street, unlike the gated driveway Madison had pulled into. A code was required for clients to access the grounds of the Big House.

A white panel van was parked in the driveway, and a man in an all-white uniform jumped out, waving to catch Derron's attention.

"Hello, there!" he said. "I'm glad I caught you.

I was afraid I had missed you."

Derron frowned. Madison hadn't mentioned any technicians or workers coming so late in the afternoon. "Are you with the exterminators? Weren't you just here?"

"Yeah, but I left a cannister in the back. Mind if I just jog around and get it?"

Derron glanced down at his watch. He had plans to meet friends at *Rainbow Bridge* in College Station and show off his new yellow sweater. He had actually worked until closing time today and was now running late for his night out.

The uniformed man noticed him consulting his watch. "It will only take a second," he promised. "I can even lock the gate behind me. My boss will have my hide if I don't bring this back tonight."

"Okay, yeah, sure," Derron decided. That yellow sweater was calling him. "Be sure the gate shuts behind you."

"Hey, man, I appreciate this," the man said as Derron held the gate open for him. "I promise to be in and out in a flash. Have a good evening."

"I plan to," Derron said with a flirty smile.

The moment Madison opened the kitchen door, a delicious aroma welcomed her inside. She was surprised to see Samuel, Patty, and Bethani busily at work.

"What is that divine smell?" Madison asked. "And what are you three doing?"

Samuel turned his scarred face toward her

with a smile. "Patty and I are cooking dinner to show our appreciation for all your family has done for us. Bethani offered to make dessert."

"Strawberry Shortcake. The easy version, of course," Bethani grinned, indicating the angel food cake she tore into small pieces and tossed into a pretty glass bowl.

"Wow. That's so nice of you. And so appreciated." Madison set her bag near the door and perched herself on a bar stool. "I've had quite a day," she confessed. "Give me a minute to catch my breath, and I'll help."

"No need. Patty and I have everything under control."

It was nice to see the easy rapport between the father and daughter. Madison was sure it wasn't easy to build a relationship practically from scratch, but they were clearly trying.

"Plus, this is sort of a farewell dinner," Patty added.

"Oh?"

Samuel nodded. "The DA's office called. They've made arrangements for us to stay closer to the courthouse. This will be our last night here, and we wanted to do something nice for you. We can never repay you for everything you and your family have done for us, but this is a start."

"That's very thoughtful, but we were happy to help you."

"All the same, this is a start. What time will Brash be home?" he asked.

Madison consulted her watch. "Soon. He had a

few last details to handle before leaving. That should give me time to run upstairs, freshen up, and come back down to help you."

"No need. Take your time."

While Madison took the back staircase up to their bedroom suite, Patty asked her father, "How will they get us out without being seen? In case someone followed us," she clarified in a worried voice.

"They'll pose as workers, the same way Brash and I did at the inn. We'll leave in their van with no one the wiser."

"That could work, I guess."

"It will," her father assured her with a smile. "How's that looking in the oven?"

Patty opened the door and peered inside. "Cheese is getting melty."

"You can turn off the oven and leave it sitting inside. It will cook within itself until we take it out."

"Where did you learn to make this, anyway? It looks amazing," the young woman said.

"I worked odd jobs through the years. I took a stab at working in a restaurant for a while. I even trained as a sous chef."

"Nice."

Even before Madison opened the door at the bottom of the stairs—having originally been the servant's passage, the stairway was discreetly tucked away from view—her stomach growled in appreciation. The air smelled so heavenly, she almost opened her mouth to taste it.

Her watch vibrated with a message that the

door to her office had opened and closed. *Derron actually worked overtime? I'm impressed,* she mused.

Until her thoughts soured. *Probably means he wants to take tomorrow off.*

"Okay, I'm back," she announced. "What can I do?"

"If you insist on helping, you can set the table."

"I do." She smiled.

"I'm putting the shortcake into the fridge to chill," Bethani said. "Let's not forget it."

"Not a chance!" Patty laughed. "It's almost too pretty to eat, but I will, anyway."

"That's what it's—" Bethani turned around, stopping abruptly. "Whoa. Who are you?"

Madison looked up to see who she spoke to. Her heart raced when she saw a strange man standing in her kitchen, wearing a nondescript white uniform and cap.

"Oh," Samuel said to the unexpected newcomer. "You must be with the extrication team. You're early."

"Change of plans," the man said brusquely.

"We weren't expecting you until tomorrow. I think our bags are packed, but we haven't eaten yet. We prepared a farewell dinner for our gracious hosts."

"It's a farewell dinner, all right."

Madison gasped when she saw a flash of metal. "Why do you have a gun?" she asked in alarm. "Who are you? And how did you get in this house? Or passed the armed gate?"

"Who I am doesn't matter. And some prissy

little fellow let me in through the gate. Thought I was the exterminator." His short laugh turned deadly. "Which," he said, pointing his gun at Roberts, "I suppose I am."

Samuel Roberts' words were more of a resigned statement than a question. "You're one of Tar-Go's goons, aren't you?"

"You didn't really think you'd slip past us, did you? We have too much riding on your testimony. Which the jury will never hear, because you'll be shark bait. We already have a boat waiting."

"As a precaution," Roberts told him in a steady voice, "the DA recorded my testimony and sworn deposition."

"Without a live witness to confirm your claim, it's all hearsay," the uniformed man said.

"Except for the evidence I have."

"Which I'm about to collect. Hand it over, Roberts."

"Do I strike you as an idiot? It's in safekeeping."

"Get it for me. I promise to make your death quick and easy. If you don't cooperate, we'll drop you off in the ocean and let the sharks tear you apart."

"Never."

The man grabbed Patty by the arm, hauling her in close to him. "I think you may have a change of heart," he sneered. "That, or we could give the sharks a true feast. Two bodies at once."

"Let my daughter go. She's got nothing to do with this."

"I'll make a trade. The information for her

life."

The other man shook his scarred face. "It won't matter. The DA already has a copy."

"I don't believe you."

"You came here for me. Let my daughter go. No need for bloodshed. I'll go with you quietly."

"You'll both go," the man decided. He shoved Patty forward, the gun in her back. "One false move, and she's dead. Now, lead the way out of here. Same way I came in."

"I don't know which way that was."

"Through the office."

"That doesn't help. I don't know the house."

"Fine. We'll all go. Ladies, lead the way." He motioned to Madison and Bethani with his gun. "March!"

Madison placed herself between Bethani and the armed man. As her daughter led the way across the sprawling house, Madison looked for ways to escape. There were multiple secret passages running through the mansion, but no way to reach them without the man seeing. Even if they scattered and ran, they couldn't all escape. He would surely shoot them before they went far.

She could grab the first heavy object they passed, but then what? Patty and Samuel were between her and the man. Madison knew she wasn't that good of an aim to lodge the missile and hit him in the head.

That left Brash. Brash would have to rescue them.

Brash turned onto Second Street, thankful to have the day over and done with. He needed food and a hot shower.

Seeing the white van in the driveway, he frowned. They didn't have anyone scheduled to do maintenance on the house today, especially this late in the afternoon. His senses went on alert. With Roberts in the house and Tar-Go willing to go to any lengths to find him, he wasn't taking any chances.

He parked behind the van, hoping to at least block their exit. He proceeded on foot, unlocking the gate and moving cautiously across the lawn.

At first glance, nothing looked out of place.

Until he saw the office door open, and Bethani stepped onto the porch. Her face was pale, and she looked frightened.

Brash ducked for cover. He needed to assess the situation before he walked into an ambush. Maddy followed their daughter out, with Roberts behind her. Next came Patty. All four of them wore tight expressions on their faces.

And with no wonder. An unfamiliar man dressed in a white uniform followed closely behind Patty. Brash couldn't see a weapon from his vantage point, but he knew the man had one and knew he had taken them hostage.

"Walk faster," the man barked. "I ain't got all day."

Bethani deliberately turned right, toward the front of the house and the walkway that connected the ornate foot gate to the mansion's main door.

"Not that way, stupid!" the man snapped.

"Toward the van."

"I'm not stupid!" she objected.

Madison heard the unmistakable call of a hoot owl. She discreetly glanced around, instinctively knowing it was Brash. It was a signal; she was certain of it.

With a mumbled apology, she reached out and gave her daughter a shove. It wasn't hard, but enough to make the girl stumble. Madison followed suit, throwing herself on Bethani so that they both tumbled to the ground. "Sorry, sweetheart," she whispered. "Stay down."

Following close on their heels, Roberts, too, stumbled. He threw his body to the left, trying hard not to land on top of them.

It gave Brash the opening he needed. The uniformed man was distracted by the trainwreck derailing in front of him. Brash rushed him from behind, striking the back of the man's head with the butt of his service weapon.

It wasn't hard enough. The man stumbled, releasing Patty and wheeling toward his attacker.

"Drop the gun!" Brash ordered.

The man ignored the directive. When he would have fired at the officer, Brash shot his upper arm. The man yelped in pain as his gun fell away. Brash pounced on him, tackling him to the ground and making quick work of handcuffing his wrists behind his back.

"Hurry, you two," he told the Roberts. "Get back in the house before someone sees you."

"Doesn't matter." The man turned his head

enough to snarl the words from his prone position. "They're dead. If not by me, someone else."

Brash fished the man's phone from his pocket. "Maddy, you and Beth okay?" he asked.

"Just shaken up." Madison helped Bethani to her feet. "Honey, you go inside. Check on Patty and Samuel. Call the station, tell them we had an intruder, and to send backup."

Brash tossed Madison the man's phone. "Scroll down and find his last call."

A quick look was all it took to report, "All the incoming and outgoing calls are to the same number."

"Probably a burner," Brash nodded, "and that's his boss. Send a text. Say something vague, like 'done.'"

Madison did as she was told, reading him the immediate response. *"Did you get the proof?"*

Madison tapped out a message and read it to Brash for approval. *"He was bluffing, or info died with him."*

"Sounds good," her husband said.

From the ground, the man blustered, "You'll never get away with this. They'll come looking for me. And when they do, you're all dead!"

Instead of being threatened, Brash sounded amused. "I think a job like this calls for a vacation, don't you, Maddy?"

"Oh, absolutely." She tapped on the keys again and read what she had typed. "Job harder than thought. Going off grid for a few days."

The man glared up at them.

"When Officer Perry gets here, we'll get him down to the station and make sure he's locked up," Brash told his wife. "The only vacation view he'll get is through bars."

27

With the events of the past two weeks behind them, Brash packed a picnic and a blanket and treated his wife to a river-therapy session.

Once they were seated on the crest of the steep red banks, he said, "Okay, you know how this works. Pick your vessel."

Madison spotted a long, sturdy limb coming around the bend. "That one," she pointed.

"Okay. What are you putting on it? What's one of your worries?"

"I worry about Samuel Roberts and Patty. I know he has proof—"

"And in the most unlikely of places," Brash chuckled. "I couldn't believe it when he pointed to his neck, laughed, and said, 'What's one more scar?' Who would ever believe he had a micro drive implanted into him?"

"Ingenious, that's for sure. But what if Tar-Go comes after him again, even after the trial?"

"What if they don't?" he countered.

"I guess they try to reunite their family and

live a somewhat normal life again."

"We've done everything we can to help that happen, Maddy," he said gently. "The rest is out of our hands. Let it go. Let that worry float away."

Together, they watched as the limb twisted, turned, and eventually carried that burden down the Brazos.

"Next?" he asked.

"Ella Getty."

Brash scanned the water before pointing his finger. "How about that log there?"

"Okay," she agreed.

"What's your specific worry?"

"I can't help but worry about her and what will happen now. A crime was committed, but it was so long ago, and in her sister's defense."

"The first crime, anyway," he pointed out.

"But there's no proof that the baby didn't die of natural causes. For all we know, it's something else Ella made up. Some of her stories may have checked out, but a lot of them were too farfetched to be true."

"Again, it's out of our hands. She'll get the psychiatric care she needs. They'll help sort out what's real and what's imagined. And if they don't, I still can't imagine her being punished after all these years. Like you said, there's no real proof to either crime."

"Best of all, her girls are rallying around her. That's what she needs the most."

"I agree."

Madison lay her head on his shoulder. Her

expression was still troubled.

"I know there's something else," he told her. "That's what we're here for. To get it out and let it go."

She sighed. "I need a really big log for this one," Madison admitted.

It took several minutes before a suitable log came down the river.

"Is that one big enough?"

"I'll try. If I can't pile it all on one log, I'll find another."

"Load 'er up, then."

Brash wasn't surprised when she loaded the log with her biggest worry of all. "The kids."

"What about them, sweetheart?"

"What if... what if we didn't do our jobs as parents, and they pay the price for our inadequacies?"

"Have they yet? You got the twins through the terrible twos, didn't you?"

"Barely!"

"I don't see any missing limbs or appendages," he teased. "No major scars. I think you did a fine job of getting them through their entire childhood. The last time I checked, Megan was fully intact, too."

"But we won't be there to protect them when they go off to college."

"Or when they drive in a car, or go to school every day, or play sports, or walk down the stairs, for that matter. We're past the point of holding their hands every day, Maddy, and guiding them to safety. We have to let them walk on their own now."

"But—"

"No buts. Our children are eighteen now. Yes, they still need us. They'll always need us. But now they'll come to us for advice, not punishment. This is their chance to prove themselves to the world and to us. To themselves. We can't deny them that privilege, sweetheart. It's a rite of passage. The bridge from dependent childhood to independent adulthood. They'll be okay."

"How do you know that?" she wailed.

"Because all three of them are smart. They know how to think for themselves and make good decisions. Sure, they'll make mistakes. Some of those mistakes will be real whoppers," Brash predicted. "But we all make mistakes. That's how we learn."

"But I'm going to miss them so much. You've gotten used to co-parenting with Shannon. Megan hasn't lived in your house every single day for the last eighteen years."

He looked down at her with reproach. "Doesn't mean I don't miss her when she's with her mother."

"I didn't mean to imply that. It's just that... I'm afraid I won't know what to do without them."

"Well, then, let's talk about the things you *won't* do without them at home." He put his arms around her and pulled her to sit against his chest.

He started. "You won't have to do mounds of laundry. You won't have to put up with Blake's smelly socks and uniforms."

"Well, there is that," she said with a small smile.

"You won't have to learn the words to every single cheer on this earth, because our girls won't be there to chant them at the top of their lungs each and every day."

"And that."

"You won't have to listen to petty arguments and name calling, or those silly pranks they like to pull on each other."

"True."

"You won't have to overstock the pantry whenever there's a sale at the grocery store, just to get us through one of Blake's hunger spells. No more stashing pasta and extra chips in the washroom."

"You found that?"

"Along with the ketchup," he said with a nod. "I was looking for laundry detergent. Which we were out of, by the way, because Megan used the last of it and forgot to tell anyone."

"As big as my pantry is, not to mention the extra butler's pantry, there's never enough room."

"See? You'll be saving on the grocery bill *and* storage."

"Maybe."

"No more juggling schedules, trying to fit in Blake's game, the girls' cheer meet, a Project Graduation meeting, and both of our work responsibilities in the same afternoon."

"I suppose there will be some advantages."

Brash snuggled his face in the crook of her neck. "I think there will be a lot of advantages to having the house to ourselves."

"And we could go on more trips. Maybe not to

Spain," she conceded, "but on an occasional getaway."

"Without having to do some major coordinating," he pointed out.

"I guess maybe I'm overreacting," Madison admitted.

"You're acting like any good, loving mother with her children's best interest at heart," he assured her. "And Maddy?"

"Yeah?"

"Look at your log now. Floating along just fine and almost around the bend. It made it, sweetheart, just like we will."

"Around the bend," she agreed softly, "and off to new adventures."

"The same thing we'll do, Maddy." He gave her a warm squeeze. "You know the saying. Come along with me, the best is yet to be."

The next great adventure for Madison and Brash begins here: Play for Dollars, Play for Death.

Note From Author

Thank you so much for reading my book. If

you have enjoyed it, please let others know by leaving a review on Amazon, BookBub, and other sites of your choice.

Reach out to me at www.beckiwillis.com or shoot me an email at beckiwillis.ccp@gmail.com.

ABOUT THE AUTHOR

Best-selling indie author Becki Willis loves crafting stories with believable characters in believable situations. Many of her stories stem from her travels and from personal experiences. (No worries; she's never actually murdered anyone).

When she's not plotting danger and adventure for her imaginary friends, Becki enjoys reading, antiquing (aka junking), unraveling a good mystery (real or imagined), dark chocolate, and a good cup of coffee. A professed history geek, Becki often weaves pieces of the past into her novels. Family is a central theme in her stories and in her life. She and her husband enjoy traveling but believe coming home to their Texas ranch is the best part of any trip.

Becki has won numerous awards, but believes the real compliments come from her readers. Drop in for an e-visit anytime at beckiwillis.ccp@gmail.com, or www.beckiwillis.com.